The Boys Next Door

The Boys Next Door

JENNIFER ECHOLS

Simon Pulse
New York London Toronto Sydney

SIMON PULSE
An imprint of Simon & Schuster Children's Publishing Division
1230 Avenue of the Americas, New York, NY 10020

Designed by Ann Zeak
The text of this book was set in Garamond 3.
Manufactured in the United States of America
First Simon Pulse edition June 2007
10 9 8 7 6
Library of Congress Control Number 2007922564
ISBN-13: 978-1-4169-1831-8
ISBN-10: 1-4169-1831-0

For my brother

Acknowledgments

Heartfelt thanks to my wonderful editor, Michelle Nagler, and my friends who helped make this book possible: Nephele Tempest, Victoria Dahl, Catherine Chant, Marley Gibson, and Caren Johnson.

Thanks also to everyone who sent me an e-mail or MySpace message saying you enjoyed *Major Crush*. You went out of your way to do this, and I appreciate it so much! You keep me afloat.

One

Sean smiled down at me, his light brown hair glinting golden in the sunlight. He shouted over the noise of the boat motor and the wind, "Lori, when we're old enough, I want you to be my girlfriend." He didn't even care the other boys could hear him.

"I'm there!" I exclaimed, because I was nothing if not coy. All the boys ate out of my hand, I tell you. "When will we be old enough?"

His blue eyes, lighter than the bright blue sky behind him, seemed to glow in his tanned face. He answered me, smiling. At least, I *thought* he answered me. His lips moved.

"I didn't hear you. What'd you say?" I know how to draw out a romantic moment.

He spoke to me again. I still couldn't hear him, though the boat motor and the wind hadn't gotten any louder. Maybe he was just mouthing words, pretending to say something sweet I couldn't catch. Boys were like that. He'd just been teasing me all along—

"You ass!" I sat straight up in my sweat-soaked bed, wiping away the strands of my hair stuck to my wet face. Then I realized what I'd said out loud. "Sorry, Mom," I told her photo on my bedside table. But maybe she hadn't heard me over my alarm clock blaring Christina Aguilera, "Ain't No Other Man."

Or maybe she'd understand. I'd just had a closer encounter with Sean! Even if it *was* only in my dreams.

Usually I didn't remember my dreams. Whenever my brother, McGillicuddy, was home from college, he told Dad and me at breakfast what he'd dreamed about the night before. Lindsay Lohan kicking his butt on the sidewalk after he tried to take her picture (pure fantasy). Amanda Bynes dressed as the highway patrol, pulling him over to give him a traffic ticket. I was jealous. I didn't want to dream about Lindsay Lohan or getting my butt kicked. However, if I was spending the night with Patrick Dempsey and didn't even *know* it, I was missing out on a very worthy third of my life. I had once Googled "dreaming" and found out some people don't remember their dreams if their bodies are used to getting up at the same hour every morning and have plenty of time to complete the dream cycle.

So why'd I remember my dream this morning? It was the first day of summer vacation, that's why. To start work at the marina, I'd set my clock thirty minutes earlier than during the school year. Lo and behold, here was my dream. About Sean: check. Blowing me off, as usual: noooooooo! That might happen in my dreams, but it wasn't going to happen in real life. Not again. Sean would be mine, starting today. I gave Mom on my beside table an okay sign—the wakeboarding signal for *ready to go*—before rolling out of bed.

My dad and my brother suspected nothing, ho ho. They didn't even notice what I was wearing. Our conversation at breakfast was the same one we'd had every summer morning since my brother was eight years old and I was five.

Dad to brother: "You take care of your sister today."

Brother, between bites of egg: "Roger that."

Dad to me: "And you watch out around those boys next door."

Me: (Eye roll.)

Brother: "I had this rockin' dream about Anne Hathaway."

Post-oatmeal, my brother and I trotted across our yard and the Vaders' yard to the complex of showrooms, warehouses, and docks at Vader's Marina. The morning air was already thick with the heat and humidity and the smell of cut grass that would last the entire Alabama summer. I didn't mind. I liked the heat. And I quivered in my flip-flops at the prospect of another whole summer with Sean. I'd been going through withdrawal.

In past years, any one of the three Vader boys, including Sean, might have shown up at my house at any time to throw the football or play video games with my brother. They might let me play too if they felt sorry for me, or if their mom had guilted them into it. And my brother might go to their house at any time. But *I* couldn't go to their house. If I'd walked in, they would have stopped what they were doing, looked up, and wondered what I was doing there. They were my brother's friends, not mine.

Well, Adam was my friend. He was probably more my friend than my brother's. Even though we were the same age, I didn't have any classes with him at school, so you'd think he'd walk a hundred yards over to my house for a visit every once in a while. But he didn't. And if I'd gone to visit him, it would have been obvious I was looking for Sean out the corner of my eye the whole time.

For the past nine months, with my brother off at college, my last tie to Sean had been severed. He was two years older than me, so I didn't have any classes with *him*, either. I wasn't even in the same wing of the high school. I saw him once at a football game, and once in front of the movie theater when I'd ridden around with Tammy for a few minutes after a tennis match. But I never approached him. He was always flirting with Holly Chambliss or Beige Dupree or whatever glamorous girl he was with at the moment. I was too young for him, and he never even thought of hooking up with me. On the very rare occasion when he took the garbage to the road at the same time I walked to the mailbox, he gave me the usual beaming smile and a big hug and acted like I was his best friend ever . . . for thirty heavenly seconds.

It had been a long winter. *Finally* we were back to the summer. The Vaders always needed extra help at the marina during the busy season from Memorial Day to Labor Day. Just like last year, I had a job there—and an excuse to make Sean my captive audience. I sped up my trek across the pine needles between the trees and found myself in a footrace against my brother. It was totally unfair because I was carrying my backpack and he was wearing sneakers, but I beat him to the warehouse by half a length anyway.

The Vader boys had gotten there before us and claimed the good jobs, so I wouldn't have a chance to work side by side with Sean. Cameron was helping the full-time workers take boats out of storage. He wanted my brother to work with him so they could catch up on their lives at two different colleges. Sean and Adam were already gone, delivering the boats to customers up and down the lake for Memorial Day weekend. Sean wasn't around to see my outfit. I was so desperate to get going on this "new me" thing, I would have settled for a double take from Adam or Cameron.

All I got was Mrs. Vader. Come to think of it, she was a good person to run the outfit by. She wore stylish clothes, as far as I could tell. Her blonde pinstriped hair was cut to flip up in the back. She looked exactly like you'd want your mom to look so as not to embarrass you in public. I found her in the office and hopped onto a stool behind her. Looking over her shoulder as she typed on the computer, I asked, "Notice anything different?"

She tucked her pinstriped hair behind her ear and squinted at the screen. "I'm using the wrong font?"

"Notice anything different about my boobs?"

That got her attention. She whirled around in her chair and peered at my chest. "You changed your boobs?"

"I'm *showing* my boobs," I said proudly, moving my palm in front of them like presenting them on a TV commercial. All this can be yours! Or, rather, your son's.

My usual summer uniform was the outgrown clothes Adam had given me over the years: jeans, which I cut off into shorts and wore with a wide belt to hold up the waist, and T-shirts from his football team. Under that, for wakeboarding in the afternoon, I used to wear a one-piece sports bathing suit with full coverage that reached all the way up to my neck. Early in the boob-emerging years, I had no boobs, and I was touchy about it. Remember in middle school algebra class, you'd type 55378008 on your calculator, turn it upside down, and hand it to the flat-chested girl across the aisle? I was that girl, you bi-yotch. I would have died twice if any of the boys had mentioned my booblets.

Last year, I thought my boobs had progressed quite nicely. And I progressed from the one-piece into a tankini. But I wasn't quite ready for any more exposure. I didn't want the boys to treat me like a girl.

Now I did. So today I'd worn a cute little bikini. Over that, I still wore Adam's cutoff jeans. Amazingly, they looked sexy, riding low on my hips, when I traded the football T-shirt for a pink tank that ended above my belly button and hugged my figure. I even had a little cleavage. I was so proud. Sean was going to love it.

Mrs. Vader stared at my chest, perplexed. Finally she said, "Oh, I get it. You're trying to look hot."

"*Thank* you!" Mission accomplished.

"Here's a hint. Close your legs."

I snapped my thighs together on the stool. People always scolded me for sitting like a boy. Then I slid off the stool and stomped to the door in a huff. "Where do you want me?"

She'd turned back to the computer. "You've got gas."

Oh, goody. I headed out the office door, toward the front dock to man the gas pumps. This meant at some point during the day, one of the boys would look around the marina office and ask, "Who has gas?" and another boy would answer, "Lori has gas." If I were really lucky, Sean would be in on the joke.

The office door squeaked open behind me. "Lori," Mrs. Vader called. "Did you want to talk?"

Nooooooo. Nothing like that. I'd only gone into her office and tried to start a conversation. Mrs. Vader had three sons. She didn't know how to talk to a girl. My mother had died in a boating accident alone on the lake when I was four. I didn't know how to talk to a woman. Any convo between Mrs. Vader and me was doomed from the start.

"No, why?" I asked without turning around. I'd been galloping down the wooden steps, but now I stepped very carefully, looking down, as if I needed to examine every footfall so I wouldn't trip.

"Watch out around the boys," she warned me.

I raised my hand and wiggled my fingers, toodle-dee-doo, dismissing her. Those boys were harmless. Those boys had better watch out for *me*.

Really, aside from the specter of the boys discussing my intestinal problems, I enjoyed having gas. I got to sit on the dock with my feet in the water and watch the kingfishers and the herons glide low over the surface. Later I'd swim on the side of the dock upriver from the gasoline. Not *now*, before Sean saw me for the first time that summer. I would be in and out of the lake and windy boats all day, and my hair would look like hell. That was understood. But I wanted to have clean, dry, styled hair at least the *first* time he saw me, and I would hope he kept the memory alive. I might go swimming *after* he saw me, while I waited around for people to drive up to the gas pumps in their boats.

The richer they were, the more seldom they made it down from Birmingham to their million-dollar vacation homes on the lake, and the more likely they were complete dumbasses when it came to docking their boats and finding their gas caps. If I covered for their dumbassedness in front of their families in the boats by giggling and saying things like, "Oh sir, I'm so sorry, *I'm* supposed to be helping *you*!" while I helped them, they tipped me beyond belief.

I was just folding a twenty into my back pocket when Sean and Adam came zipping across the water in the boat emblazoned with VADER'S MARINA down the side, blasting Nickelback from the speakers. They turned hard at the edge of the idle zone. Three-foot swells shook the floating dock violently and would have shaken me off into the water if I hadn't held on to the rail. Then the bow of the boat eased against the padding on the dock. Adam must be the one driving. Sean would have driven all the way to the warehouse, closer to where they'd pick up the next boat for delivery.

In fact, as Sean threw me the rope to tie the stern and Adam cut the engine, I could hear them arguing about this. Sean and Adam argued pretty much 24/7. I was used to it. But I would rather not have heard Sean complaining that they were going to have to walk a whole extra fifty yards and up the stairs just so Adam could say hi to me.

Sean jumped off the boat. His weight rocked the floating dock again as he tied up the bow. He was big, maybe six feet tall, with a deep tan from working all spring at the marina, and a hard, muscled chest and arms from competing with Adam the last five years over who could lift more poundage on the dumbbell in their garage (Sean and Adam were like this). Then he straightened and smiled his beautiful smile at me, and I forgave him everything.

Two

"Hey, Buddy," he said to me. I got a close-up view of his strange, light blue eyes and golden skin as he threw his arms around me and kept walking right over me. I had to throw my arms around him, too, to keep from thudding flat on my back on the dock.

"Oh pardon me!" he said, pulling me out from under him and setting me on my feet again. "I didn't even see you there."

"That's quite all right," I managed in the same fake-formal tone. His warm hands still held my waist. This was the first time a boy had every touched my bare tummy. My happy skin sent shocked messages to my brain that went something like, *He's touching me! Are you getting this? He's touching me!*

Eeeeeeee! My brain got it, all right, and put the rest of my body on high alert. My heart thumped painfully, just like in my dream.

But as I looked into his eyes, I saw he was already gone, glancing up the stairs to the marina. If I didn't know better, I'd say he'd been flirting with me. I knew better. He treated all girls this way.

He slid out of my grasp. He may have had to shake one hand violently to extricate it from my friendly vise-like grip. "See you later, Junior," he threw over his shoulder at me as he climbed the steps to the marina.

When we were kids, he'd started calling my brother *McGillicuddy* because he thought our last name was such a riot. It caught on with the other Vader boys, and Cameron had told everyone at school. I'm not sure anyone in town knew my brother as Bill. Thankfully, everyone in town knew me as Lori. The names Sean had made up for me were too long to be practical nicknames: McGillicuddy Junior, McGillicuddy the Younger, McGillicuddy Part Deux, McGillicuddy Returns, McGillicuddy Strikes Back, McGillicuddy's Buddy.

You see what I was up against? Obviously he still saw me as my brother's little sister. I sighed, watching him climb the steps, muscles moving underneath the tan skin of his legs. He was immune to the delicious temptation of my pink tank top. But I had another trick up my sleeve, or lack thereof. Later that afternoon, when we went wakeboarding, I would initiate Stage Two: Bikini.

The dock dipped again as Adam jumped from the boat. I turned to greet him. We did our secret handshake, which we'd been adding to for years: the basic shake (first grade), upside down (second grade), with a twist (fourth grade), high five (fifth grade), low five (seventh grade), pinky swear (eighth grade), elbows touching (ninth grade). We'd been known to do the secret handshake when we passed in the halls at school, and on the sidelines during Adam's football games.

Everybody on the girls' tennis team fetched water and bandages for the football team during their games. It wasn't fair. The football team didn't bring *us* drinks and bandages at tennis tournaments. I never complained, though, because I got to stand on the football field where the action was, which was all I really wanted. The secret handshake had proven surprisingly hard to do when Adam was in football pads. We'd made it work.

But Adam had gotten together with Rachel a month before. Ever since I'd heard a rumor that she didn't want her boyfriend doing the secret handshake with "that 'ho next door," I'd tried to cool it in public. I mean, if *I'd* had a boyfriend, I wouldn't have wanted him doing a secret handshake with anybody but me, especially if he looked like Adam.

Because Adam looked basically like Sean. Up close and in daylight, you'd never mistake them for each other, especially now that they were older. Their facial features were different. At a distance or in the dark, all bets were off.

Adam's hair was longer than Sean's and always in his eyes, but you couldn't tell this when they were both windblown in the extreme, like now. If you happened to be watching them from your bedroom window as they got in a fight and beat the crap out of each other at the edge of their yard where their mom couldn't see them from their house—not that I would ever do such a thing—you could tell them apart only because Sean was more filled out and a little taller, since he was two years older. Also, they walked differently: Sean cruised suavely, while Adam bounced like the ball that got away from you and led you into the street after it.

But what I always looked for to tell them apart instantly, when I could see it, was Adam's skull-and-crossbones pendant on a leather cord. I'd bought the pendant from a bubblegum machine when we were twelve. In one of my many failed attempts over the years to become more girl-like, I'd been trying for a Mary-Kate and Ashley pendant for myself. The last thing I wanted was a skull and crossbones. I'd given it to Adam because it was made for him.

Suddenly I realized I was standing on the hot wood of the dock, still touching elbows with Adam, staring at the skull-and-crossbones pendant. And when I looked up into his light blue eyes, I saw that *he* was staring at *my* neck. No. Down lower.

"What'cha staring at?" I asked.

He cleared his throat. "Tank top or what?" This was his seal of approval, as in, *Last day of school or what?* or, *Dallas Cowboys Cheerleaders or what?* Hooray! He wasn't

Sean, but he was built of the same material. This was a good sign.

I pumped him for more info, to make sure. "What *about* my tank top?"

"You're wearing it." He looked out across the lake, showing me his profile. His cheek had turned bright red under his tan. I had embarrassed *the wrong boy*. Damn, it was back to the football T-shirt for me.

No it wasn't, either. I couldn't abandon my plan. I had a fish to catch.

"Look," I told Adam, as if he hadn't already looked. "Sean's leaving at the end of the summer. Yeah, yeah, he'll be back next summer, but I'm afraid I won't be able to compete once he's had a taste of college life and sorority girls. It's now or never, and desperate times call for desperate tank tops."

Adam opened his mouth to say something. I shut him up by raising my hand. Imitating his deep boy-voice, I said, "I don't know why you want to hook up with that jerk." We'd had this conversation whenever we saw each other lately. I said in my normal voice, "I just do, okay? Let me do it, and don't get in my way. Stay out of my net, little dolphin." I bumped his hip with my hip. Or tried to, but he was a lot taller than me. I actually hit somewhere around his mid-thigh.

He folded his arms, stared me down, and pressed his lips together. He tried to look grim. I could tell he was struggling not to laugh. "Don't call me that."

"Why not?"

"Dolphins don't live in the lake," he said matter-of-factly, as if this were the real reason. The real reason was that the man-child within him did not want to be called "little" anything. Boys were like that.

I shrugged. "Fine, little brim. Little bass."

He walked toward the stairs.

"Little striper."

He turned. "What if Sean actually asked you out?"

I didn't want to be *teased* about this. It could happen! "You act like it's the most remote poss—"

"He has to ride around with the sunroof open just so he can fit his big head in the truck. Where would you sit?"

"In his lap?"

A look of disgust flashed across Adam's face before he jogged up the stairs, his weight making the weathered planks creak with every step. I wasn't really worried he would ruin things for me and Sean, though. Adam and I had always gotten along great. When the older boys picked on us, we stood up for each other as best we could. The idea of me hooking up with Sean bothered him simply because he hated Sean with the white heat of a thousand suns, and the feeling was mutual.

A few minutes later, just as I was helping the clueless captain of a ski boat shove off, I heard footsteps on the stairs behind me. Sean alert! Sensory overload! But no, I saw from the skull-and-crossbones pendant that it was Adam.

On cue, Sean puttered past us in a powerful boat, blasting Crossfade instead of Nickelback for a little variety, looking so powerful himself in cool sunglasses, his tanned chest polished by the sun. He waited until he reached the very edge of the idle zone (Mr. Vader was probably watching from somewhere inside the marina to make sure the boys idled in the idle zone) and floored it across the lake to make another delivery.

I'd forgotten all about Adam behind me until he tickled my ribs. In fact, I was so startled, I would have fallen in the lake if he hadn't caught me. This was the second time ever a boy had touched my bare tummy, and something of an anticlimax.

Don't get me wrong—the attention and his fingers on my skin were very pleasant. But he was just being friendly, brotherly. He was totally devoted to Rachel, and he knew I was totally devoted to Sean. It was like craving a doughnut and getting french fries. You were left with an odd taste in your mouth, and you still wanted that doughnut afterward.

Mmmmm, doughnut.

For the rest of the morning, I pumped gas. I worked on my baby tan through the SPF 45. At lunchtime I went up to the marina and ate the chicken salad sandwich Mrs. Vader made me and watched *What Not to Wear*, which I'd been studying recently almost as hard as I'd studied for my algebra final this week. I ate veeeeeeeeery slowly, one nibble of bread and scrap of celery at a time, in case the beginning of Sean's lunch coincided with the end of mine.

After Mrs. Vader looked in on me the fourteenth time, I got the hint and galloped back down to the gas pumps. Of course *that's* when Sean and Adam roared back into the marina in the boat.

I gave up. Now that Sean had seen me dry, it was safe to go swimming. *Safe* being a relative term. I knew from experience that before you went swimming off a dock for the first time each summer, you needed to check the sides and the ladder carefully for bryozoa, colonies of slimy green critters that grew on hard surfaces underwater (think coral, but gelatinous—*shudder*). They wouldn't hurt you, they were part of a healthy freshwater ecosystem, their presence meant the water was pristine and unpolluted, blah blah blah—but none of this was any consolation if you accidentally *touched them*. Poking around with a water ski and finding nothing, I spent the rest of the afternoon watching for Sean from the water.

And getting out occasionally when he sped by in the boat, in order to woo him like Halle Berry coming out of the ocean in a James Bond movie (which I had seen with the boys about a hundred times. Bikini scene, seven hundred times). Only I seemed to have misplaced my dagger.

Sometimes Sean was behind the wheel. Sometimes Adam was. I could tell which was which even when I was too far away to see the skull and crossbones. Adam was the one waving to me, and Sean was the one looking hot behind his sunglasses. Maybe Sean was watching me and I simply couldn't tell from his mysterious exterior. He only *appeared* unmoved by my newfound buxom beauty.

Yeah, probably not. There were several problems with this theory, not the least of which was that when they passed by, I never timed my exit from the water quite right for Stage Two: Bikini. Then, in case they did turn around, I had to appear as if I'd meant to get out all along—for some reason other than driving Sean to distraction with lust.

Oh—hair toss—I was getting out to look at teen fashion mags, like a normal almost-sixteen-year-old girl. I examined the pictures and checked this info against what I'd gathered from *What Not to Wear*, plus some common sense (I hoped). High fashion was all well and good, but if it prompted the object of your affection to comment that you looked pregnant or you had elf feet, really it wasn't serving its purpose.

Around four o'clock I climbed the stairs and walked around to the warehouses. I knew the boys wouldn't save me the hike by driving around to the gas pumps to pick me up. Adam might, if it were up to him, but it wasn't up to him.

Just as well. Adam, Sean, Cameron and my brother, all wearing board shorts, stood in a line, pitching wakeboards and water skis and life vests and tow ropes from the warehouse into the boat. Adam, Cameron and McGillicuddy half-turned toward Sean as he related some amusing anecdote that was probably only thirty percent true. In fact, the other boys didn't notice, but Sean had stopped working. They handed wakeboards around Sean in the line. His only job was to entertain.

I wanted him to entertain me, too. I could listen to Sean's stories forever. The way he told it, a trip to the grocery store sounded like *American Pie*. But I had a job to do. I had a grand entrance to make. While walking toward them, I dropped my backpack, then pulled my tank top off over my head to reveal my bikini.

And just balled up my tank top in one hand as if it were nothing, and threw it into the boat. "Heeeeeey!" I said in a high girl-voice as I hugged Cameron, whom I hadn't seen since he'd come home from college for the summer a few days ago. He hugged me back and kept glancing at my boobs and trying not to. My brother had that look on his face like he was going to ask Dad to take me to the shrink again.

I bent over with my butt toward them, dropped my shorts, and threw those in the boat, too. When I straightened and turned toward the boys, I was in for a shock.

I had thought I wanted Sean to stare at me. I *did* want him to stare. But now that Sean and Cameron and Adam were all staring at me, speechless, I wondered whether there was chicken salad on my bikini, or—somewhat worse—an exposed nipple.

I didn't feel a breeze down there, though. And even I, with my limited understanding of grand entrances and seducing boys, understood that if I glanced in the direction they were staring and there *were* no nipple, the effect of the grand entrance would be lost. So I snapped my fingers and asked, "Zone much?" Translation: *I'm hot? Really? Hmph.*

Adam blinked and turned to Sean. "Bikini or what?"

Sean still stared at my boobs. Slowly he

brought his strange pale eyes up to meet my eyes. "This does a lot for you," he said, gesturing to the bikini with the hand flourish of Clinton from *What Not to Wear*. Surely this was my imagination. He didn't *really* know I'd been studying how to be a girl for the past year!

"Sean," I said without missing a beat, "*I* do a lot for the *bikini*."

Cameron snorted and shoved Sean. Adam shoved him in the other direction. Sean smiled and seemed perplexed, like he was trying to think of a comeback but couldn't, for once.

Off to the side, my brother still looked very uncomfortable. I hadn't thought through how he'd react to the unveiling of the swan. I hadn't thought through *any* of their reactions very well, in case you weren't getting this. I wanted Sean to ask me out, but I didn't want to lose my relationship, such as it was, with everybody else. Like *The Price Is Right*: I wanted to come as close as I could to winning Sean without going over.

"Team calisthenics," McGillicuddy called. I understood he wanted to change the subject, but I'd hoped we could skip team calisthenics now that we were all grown up. Mr. Vader used to make us do push-ups together before we went out. The stronger we were, the less likely we were to get hurt. When my brother and Cameron got their boater's licenses and we started going out without Mr. Vader, we kept doing push-ups before every wakeboard outing. It was a good way for the rest of the boys to keep Adam and me in our places.

No hesitation, no complaint—this was part of the game. I dropped on my hands on the concrete wharf just as fast as the rest of them, and started doing push-ups. All five of us did push-ups, heads close together, with limited grunting at first. And absolutely no grunting from me or from Adam. We stayed in shape, because we cared about the calisthenics.

And because we both were in training for sports. Adam might start for the football team this year. I was just trying not to get kicked off the tennis team by an incoming freshman. My game was okay, but I was nowhere near as good as Holly and Beige, who had just graduated. Or Tammy, who would be a senior this year, and team captain. Plus, there was an unfortunate incident last year. I didn't train all winter, got to our first meet, overexerted myself, and barfed on the court. I went on to win the match 6–2, 6–1, but nobody seemed to remember that part. Since then, I'd made sure to stay in shape.

Today I held my own in push-ups. After about fifty, I was nowhere near my limit. Cameron's grunting increased. I tried to concentrate on my own self, but Cameron was hard to ignore. His face turned very red. His arms trembled, and finally he collapsed on his bare stomach. My brother hadn't trembled or grunted as much, but he took the opportunity to lie down on his stomach, too, hoping no one would notice as Cameron drew the fire.

Cameron cursed and said, "I don't know why I can't get my ass in gear today."

Between push-ups, I breathed, "About twelve ounces too much frat party for both of you."

Cameron scrambled toward me. I knew I was in trouble, but it was too late to get up and run. One solid arm circled my waist. With his other arm, he held my legs so tightly I couldn't wiggle or, better yet, kick in him the gut. He took two steps toward the edge of the wharf.

I managed not to plead or scream. After almost sixteen years with boys, I had a lot of control over my natural girl-reactions. It wasn't until he pitched me off that I remembered I *did* want to react like a girl today. Then, as I hit the water, I realized I hadn't screened this swimming area for bryozoa. "Eeee—"

I plunged in. Almost before my toes hit the bottom, I was pushing up through the water, toward the sunbeams and the platform on the back of the boat, which was less likely to harbor bryozoa than any part of the concrete wharf. Ugh, ugh, ugh, I could almost feel a heinous mass squishing past my skin—but I made it safely to the surface.

And slapped myself mentally as I climbed up on the platform. If I'd pulled off my new siren act, Cameron wouldn't have tossed me into the lake. I would have been too delicate and too haughty. He wouldn't have dared to touch me. On the other hand, he did recognize that I was a girl, on some level. If I'd been Adam, he would have just shoved me in instead of picking me up.

By the time I stood on the platform, I remembered I was now wearing a *wet* bikini.

I collected myself enough to make jumping down into the boat look halfway svelte. But nobody was looking at me anymore. Cameron and my brother stood over Adam and Sean still doing push-ups.

Adam, eyes on the concrete, kept pushing himself up in an even rhythm. Sean watched Adam with a little smile and gritted teeth, turning and redder and redder. The bulging muscles of Sean's tanned arms trembled.

Oh God, Sean was going to lose.

Three

He fell on the concrete with a groan, followed by eleven choice curse words. Adam kept doing push-ups, probably because these games we played tended to change without warning. Sean might claim Adam was required to do five more push-ups per year younger. Adam was no fool. He made sure. Sean stood, and Adam was *still* doing push-ups.

"We've created a monster," my brother said.

Adam did one last push-up for good measure and stood up slowly. He clapped his hands together to brush off the dust. And then—*don't do it, Adam, don't make Sean any angrier than he already is*—he gave Sean a grin.

"I don't believe it!" shouted Cameron. "You know what else? Adam is taller! Stand back-to-back and let me make sure."

Sean refused to stand back-to-back with Adam. They goaded him and called him names that I can't repeat, but that had to do with Sean being a girl, the worst insult imaginable. So Sean and Adam stood back-to-back. Sure enough, Sean was more muscular and filled out, as always, but Adam was half an inch taller.

Adam turned and gave Sean that grim look with dropped jaw, trying not to laugh. "I'm the biggest."

"Ohhhhhh!" Cameron and my brother moaned like Adam had gotten in a good punch on Sean in one of their boxing matches. I'll spare you the full five minutes of size jokes that ensued. Tammy and some other girls on the tennis team had told me they were so jealous of me growing up around boys, because I had a window into how boys thought. This, my friends, was the deep, dark secret. The size jokes went on and on as if I weren't there, or as if I weren't a girl. I wasn't sure which was worse.

Sean smiled, wincing only a little when they shoved him. He would keep smiling no matter what they said to him. This was one of the many things I loved about Sean. Surely the boys knew they couldn't break him. They would try anyway.

I was a little concerned about what Sean would do to Adam later. Sean didn't let Adam get away with stuff like that. But I supposed that was Adam's business, the dumbass.

Disgusted, I sat in the boat with my back to them. When they ran out of size jokes for the moment—they would think of more as the afternoon went on, trust me—they piled into the boat and proceeded to argue about who got to drive first. The consensus was that Sean could drive first as a consolation prize because he was a loser.

There was no question about me driving. I got my boater's license when I turned fifteen, just like they did. The problem was that I didn't know my left from my right. This was their fault, really. They taught me to waterski when I was five years old. Nobody thought I'd get up and stay up on the first try, so I wasn't properly instructed on the dismount. I couldn't steer. Too terrified to drop the rope, I ran into the dock and broke my arm.

My *right* arm. At the time, my brain must have been designing the circuitry that told me left from right. Because since then, I'd never been able to hear Sean yell, "Go left!" or my brother holler, "Turn to the right!" without thinking, *Okay. I broke my right arm. This is my right arm. They want me to turn this way,* by which time I had missed the turn, or run the boy I was pulling on the wakeboard into a tree. We found this out the hard way last summer, the first time I tried to pull Adam.

Sean started the engine and putted through the marina waters, and Adam had the nerve to plop onto the seat across the aisle from me. Sean reached the edge of the idle zone and cranked the boat into top speed. Adam called to me so softly I could barely catch his words over the motor, "Close your legs."

"What for? I waxed!" I looked down to make sure. This was okay now, because Sean was facing the other way and couldn't hear me in the din. Indeed, I was clean. I spread my legs even wider, put my arms on the back of the seat, and generally took up as much room as possible, like a boy. I glanced back over at Adam. "Does it make you uncomfortable for me to sit this way?"

He watched me warily. "Yes."

"May I suggest that this is your problem and not mine?"

He licked his lips and bent toward me. "If it keeps Sean from asking you out, it's going to be *your* problem, and you're going to *make* it my problem."

"Speaking of which," I said, crossing my legs like a girl. "Thanks for staying out of my way. How the hell am I supposed to get Sean to ask me out when he's all pissy?"

"You wanted me to lose to him at team calisthenics? That was too sweet to miss."

"You didn't have to win by quite so much, Adam. You knew I needed him in a good mood. You didn't have to rub it in."

Adam grinned. "And you wanted me to stop growing?"

"Do *not* make a joke about your size. If you can't think of anything to talk about except your large size, please say nothing at all."

So we sat in silence until Sean slowed the boat in the middle of the lake. McGillicuddy put on his life vest, sat on the platform, slipped his feet into the bindings of his wakeboard, and hopped into the water. He and Cameron had been the ones to discover wakeboarding, and they did it first while the rest of us were still water-skiing. To look at them today, you'd think they'd never gotten the hang of it. My brother face-planted twice in his twenty-minute turn. Cameron had a hard time getting up. Frankly, I was beginning to worry.

Since we were kids, we'd spent every summer afternoon skiing and wakeboarding behind the VADER'S MARINA boat as advertisement for the business. Sean had even convinced Mr. Vader to go all out with a boat made especially for wakeboarding, which made bigger waves. Bars arched over the boat for attaching the tow rope, and speakers on the bars blasted Nickelback like the music came on automatically with the boat motor. (Once I'd brought the first Kelly Clarkson album and asked to play it rather than Nickelback while we wakeboarded. They'd laughed in my face and called me Miss Independent for months.)

We held a special wakeboarding exhibition when the lake was crowded on the Fourth of July and Labor Day. But our show during the Crappy Festival in two weeks was the most important, because sales of boats and equipment at the marina were highest near the beginning of the summer. Okay, it was actually the *Crappie* Festival. Crappie is a kind of fish, pronounced more like *croppie*. The Crappie Festival had a Crappie Queen and a Crappie Bake-Off and a Crappie Toss, in which folks competed to throw a dead fish farthest down the lake shore. Sean started calling it the Crappy Festival, which sounded a lot more fun.

But the festival would be no fun at all if we kept wakeboarding like *this*! None of us had been out on the water since Labor Day last year, but come on. I never expected Cameron and my brother to be quite so awful on their first time out. And since Sean would be watching me now, I hoped I broke the cycle.

I strapped a life vest over my bikini. Such a pity to cover my shapely body (snort). Then I tied my feet tightly into the bindings attached to my board. I hopped into the water, wakeboard and all, and assumed the position. I wished my brother would putter the boat away from me a little faster. The wakeboard floated on its side in front of me as I crouched behind it with my knees spread. Talk about needing to close my legs! The embarrassing stance had caused me to get up too quickly and face-plant more times than I cared to count, just to save myself a few seconds of the boys cracking jokes about me that I couldn't hear.

Not today. I relaxed in the water. Anyone care for an eyeful? I parted my knees and gave Adam the okay sign. He was spotting. Sean and Cameron watched me, too, as concerned as I was that we *all* sucked and Mr. Vader would pull the plug on our daily outing. No pressure. When my brother finally got around to opening up the engine, I let the boat pull me up and relaxed into the adrenalin rush.

Wakeboarding was pretty simple. I stood on the wakeboard like a skateboard, and held onto the rope as if I were waterskiing. The boat motor left a triangular wake behind it as the boat moved through the water. I moved outside it by going over one of the small waves. Then I turned back inward and used one wave as a skateboarding ramp to take off. I sailed over the wake, and used the opposite wave as a ramp to land.

After a few minutes I mostly forgot about the boys, even Sean. The drone of the motor would do that like nothing else: put me in this different zone. Even though I was connected by a rope to the boat and the outside world, I was all alone with myself. I just enjoyed the sun and the water and the wakeboard.

My intention all along had been to get my wakeboarding legs back this first day. Maybe I'd do tricks when we went out the next day. I didn't want to get too cocky and bust ass in front of Sean. But as I got more comfortable and forgot to care, I tried a few standbys—a front flip, a scarecrow. There was no busting of ass. So I tried a backroll. And landed it solidly.

Now I got cocky. I did a heelside backroll with a nosegrab. This meant that in the middle of the flip, I let go of the rope handle with one hand, reached down, and grabbed the front of the board. It served no purpose in the trick except to look impressive, like, *This only appears to be a difficult trick. I have all the time in the world. I will grab the board. Yawn.* And I landed it. This was getting too good to be true.

My brother swung the boat around just before we reached the graffiti-covered highway bridge that spanned the lake. Cameron had spray-painted his name and his girlfriend's name on the bridge, alongside all the other couples' names and over the faded ones. My genius brother had tried to paint his own name but ran out of room on that section of bridge.

McGILLICUDD
Y

Sean wisely never painted his girlfriends' names. He would have had to change them too often. For my part, I was very thankful that when most of this spray-painting action was going on last summer, I was still too short to reach over from the pile and haul myself up on the main part of the bridge. I probably had the height and the upper body strength now, and I prayed none of the boys pointed this out. Then I'd have to spray-paint LORI LOVES SEAN on the bridge. And move to Canada.

It was kind of strange Adam hadn't spray-painted his name with Rachel's in the past few weeks. Maybe he didn't consider it daring enough, if Cameron had managed to do it. Adam *had* painted in red letters in the very center of the bridge, WASH ME. The bridge was a big part of our lake experience.

Wakeboarding underneath it would have been cool. But driving the boat under the bridge while towing a wakeboarder was dangerous. Adam had been the one to discover this (seventh grade).

My brother pointed the boat for the rail. A few summers ago, the boys had pulled the guts out of an old pontoon boat that also said VADER'S MARINA down the side. They anchored it near the shore and built a rail sticking out from it, topped with PVC pipe. You could really hurt yourself on this contraption (Adam: eighth grade) but my ride was going great, and I was in the groove. I zoomed far out from the wakeboarding boat, popped up onto the rail, slid across it on the board, and landed nice and soft in the water on the other end.

Adam raised both fists at me. (Nice, but no love from Sean?) If Adam yelled, I couldn't hear him over the boat motor. What I *could* hear as my brother paralleled the shoreline was the Thompsons and the Foshees, our neighbors hanging out on their docks. They came out to watch us practice a lot of afternoons. Cha-ching! Two sales we'd as good as made for Vader's Marina when their kids got a little older.

Then came my family's dock, the Vader's dock at their house, and finally the marina. Dad had gotten home from work, I saw. He and Mr. Vader sat in lawn chairs on the marina dock, holding beers. I really shouldn't have done this if I was trying to be ladylike. But the opportunity was too perfect to resist, and old habits died hard. I arced way out from the wake, aiming for the dock.

My dad saw me coming and knew exactly what was going to happen. He jumped from his chair and jogged up the stairs, toward the shore, so I wouldn't ruin his business suit. His tie flapped over his shoulder. He didn't warn Mr. Vader, who took a sip of beer as I slid past, spraying water probably fifteen feet in the air behind me.

The wall of water smacked right on top of him. I didn't want to turn my head to look, lose my balance, fall, and ruin the effect (chicken salad on bikini, hello). But I saw him out the corner of my eye, T-shirt and shorts soaked, beer halted in midair.

Sean probably heard me cackling all the way up in the boat. Sex-y. I tried to calm myself and concentrate. I wanted to try an air raley, which I'd been working up to last summer but never landed. If there was one good reason for Sean never to ask me out, it was that he couldn't shake the memory of me wiping out after an air raley. Done correctly, I would hang in the air behind the boat for a few seconds with the board above my head. I would then sail down the opposite wake and land sweetly. Done incorrectly, it was a high-speed belly flop.

When I busted ass (or tummy), Sean and the other boys would make fun of me for the rest of the boat ride, and would spread it around their party that night. But they were so far away in the toy boat, and the drone of the motor was like a bubble around me. Nothing could hurt me in here.

I gestured upward, which told Adam to tell my brother to speed up. Adam knew what I planned to do and shook his head at me. What a pain, to stop the boat and *argue* with him about it. *He* didn't consult anyone before *he* tried a trick and busted ass. If we stopped, Sean would insist my turn was over, and I'd be done for the day. I wasn't done. So I nodded my head vigorously. Adam shook his finger at me, scolding. Then he turned around and spoke to my brother.

The drone pitched higher as the boat sped up. I relaxed, relaxed, relaxed and let the boat and the wave do the work for me. My muscles remembered what they'd tried to do last summer, and this time they were able to do it. I caught miles of air, a huge thrill, and one glance at the boat: four boys with their mouths open. Then I almost panicked as I lost my balance when my board hit its high point behind me. *Almost*—but I kept myself together. I rode gravity down the opposite wave.

Immediately I arced out and back to pick up speed, and did a 360 with a grab. Landed it. Then a 540. Landed it.

I thought I might be pushing my luck. I'd probably break my leg climbing back into the boat. Also, I didn't want my arms to be so sore the next day that I couldn't ride at all. I signaled to Adam that I was stopping and dropped the rope. The handle skipped away from me across the surface of the lake.

As the echo of the motor faded away and I sank into the warm water, I could hear them clapping for me. All four of them, standing up in the boat, facing me, applauding me and cheering for me. "Yaaaaaaay, Junior!"

I had never been so happy in my life.

And it got better.

Four

I bent over in the water to loosen the bindings, slipped my feet out, and kicked my way back to the boat with my board floating in front of me. As I pulled myself up on the platform, Sean put out one hand to help me—totally unnecessary, since I'd climbed up on the platform a thousand times before with no help.

"I taught her everything she knows," he said loudly enough for the other boys to hear, but looking only at me. He gave me his beautiful smile, a secret smile for the two of us to share, and sat down again.

"That's bullshit," Cameron said.

"I was the one who helped her most with the air raley last summer," my brother said.

"Tough act to follow," Adam told me, shrugging on his life vest. I would have treasured this comment forever if I hadn't been high on Sean.

But I was. So I peeled off my life vest and dropped it on the floor of the boat, sat daintily in the seat where Adam had been, and crossed my legs. Like my fingers had a mind of their own, they bent inward and rubbed my palm where Sean had touched me. I tingled all over again at the thought. Or maybe I tingled because my body was still jacked from how hard I'd worked my muscles out on the water. Either way, I felt so lovely and sated just then, with the sun in my eyes. I wished Adam weren't jumping in for his turn.

Because watching Adam wakeboard was not relaxing. He wasn't careful when wakeboarding. Or in general. He was the opposite of careful. His life was one big episode of *Jackass*. He would do anything on a dare, so the older boys dared him a lot. My role in this game was to run tell their mom. If I'd been able to run faster when we were kids, I might have saved Adam from a broken arm, several cracked ribs, and a couple of snake bites.

Knowing this, it might not make a lot of sense that Mr. Vader let us wakeboard for the marina. But we'd come to wakeboarding only gradually. When we first started out, it was more like, *Look at the very young children on water skis! How adorable.* One time the local newspaper ran a photo of me and Adam waterskiing double, each of us holding up an American flag. It's okay for you to gag now. I can take it.

But Mr. Vader was no fool. He understood things changed. After the second time Adam broke his collarbone, Mr. Vader put us under strict orders not to get hurt, because it was bad for business. Customers might not be so eager to buy a wakeboard and all the equipment if they witnessed our watery death. To enforce this rule, the punishment for bleeding in the boat was that we had to clean the boat. Adam cleaned the boat a lot last summer.

At the end of the rope, Adam signaled that he was ready to go. I told Cameron, who was driving now. He started too slow, and Adam tried to get up too fast. "Down," I called.

"Come on, LD," Sean muttered as if Adam were right in front of him. Even though I'd heard this joke one billion times and didn't think it was funny, I made sure to look over at Sean and laugh until he saw me laughing. He laughed too.

Adam had attention deficit disorder. This was why I didn't see a lot of him during the school year. I was in all the advanced classes, and he definitely was not. Sean had lots of fun with this. The boys actually called Adam ADD to his face. They called him LD (for Learning Disability). They called him SAS (for Short Attention Span) and Sassy and Sassafras. They told him the short bus was coming for him. He had a prescription to help him concentrate in school, but he refused to take it because it made him feel dead. In other words, he was perfectly happy with ADD. Or he *would* have been, if the boys had left him alone about it.

Sometimes I thought he took stupid risks to make up for being slow in school. Or maybe he was just like that. The skull-and-crossbones pendant was perfect for him. The boys told him if he improved his grades, when he graduated he could apply to pirate school.

Cameron brought the boat around and

straightened the rope. I told him Adam was ready to go. This time they got it right. Adam got up. Immediately he told me to speed up, and I told Cameron. Adam did a tantrum to blind, which meant he back-flipped where he couldn't see and ended with his back to the boat. He preferred tricks with a blind landing. He told me to speed up again, and I told Cameron. Adam did a turn to blind, touched down on the edge of his board, and miraculously managed not to fall.

"Good save!" McGillicuddy shouted from the front of the bow.

"Dumb luck," Sean said.

I smiled at Sean. I would feel guilty later about laughing, as I always did when I laughed at Sean's mean jokes. But while I was there with him, he was so charming, and I couldn't help but laugh.

When I looked back at Adam again, he was in the middle of a 540 to blind, which was fine, but for the love of God, he hardly had time to land before he hit the rails on the pontoon boat. I waved to get his attention, then swiped my finger across my throat: *cut it out*. He signaled for me to speed up.

I told Cameron, "Adam would like to spend this summer in traction. Speed up."

I turned back around in my seat to watch Adam again. Sean was leaning toward me in his seat, watching *me*. "Cold?" he asked me.

Pardon? Yeah, the ninety-degree afternoon and ninety-percent humidity always gave me a chill I couldn't shake. But one delicate, haughty brain cell in the back of my mind told me he was *flirting* with me and I should *feign helplessness*.

"I'm freezing!" I squealed. And just like that, Sean Vader moved across to my side of the aisle and scooted against me in my seat until I made room for him. He put his hot bare arm around my bare shoulders. And I fainted.

No, I didn't really. But I did feel dazed, perhaps from the hyperventilation. Suddenly I realized Adam had been gesturing wildly at me for several seconds without it even registering with me. He signaled me to slow down. I told Cameron.

Adam did a front flip. Sean said in my ear, "Gosh, I've never seen anyone do *that* before. Makes me want to buy a wakeboard from Vader's Marina!" I giggled. Adam signaled me to slow down more, and I told Cameron.

Adam did a back roll with a grab. Sean put his free hot hand on my bare knee and whispered, "You don't believe Adam's bigger than me, do you?"

This time I missed a beat. I was used to locker room humor. But Sean directing locker room humor at *me*, flirting with *me*? It seemed unlikely that Stage Two: Bikini had worked so quickly. Was I reading him wrong? Adam gave me the thumbs-down, and I told Cameron to slow the boat one more time.

Just as I turned back around, Adam launched into what could only be an S-bend, which was absolutely impossible to land with the boat going this slowly.

Sean, McGillicuddy and I all swore at once, and watched Adam's long, slow death-splash with interest and resignation.

"Down," I called to Cameron.

Sean gave me the funniest look that said *no shit*. I laughed out loud. He smiled again as he found his board and slipped over the back of the boat to the platform.

Adam emerged from the depths, vaulted over the side of the boat, and stood close to my seat so he dripped on my formerly comfy, sun-dried self. He commented, "S-bend or what?"

"Or what?" Cameron said. "What the hell were you doing, trying it that slow?"

"Sometimes I want to try new things," Adam said. "Sometimes I want to do things I know are bad for me, just for fun and profit. Don't you, Lori?"

I gazed way up at him and gave him a look that said, *Stay out of my net, little dolphin*. He grinned right back at me, defiant.

"Yeah, Adam," I said. "Sometimes I like to stick my finger in a light socket to see what will happen."

He pointed at me. "Exactly." Without another word to me, he took off his life vest and handed it to Sean.

Sean got up on his first try without any trouble. He never attempted any tricks he couldn't do perfectly. We always ended the exhibitions with him. We could count on him to do impressive moves, but nothing he couldn't land.

That's why I watched in disbelief when, after a few textbook flips, he launched an air raley. Surely he wasn't doing it just because *I'd* landed one. Or maybe he was, and this was his way of teasing me. Anything I could do, he could do better.

Except he couldn't. He panicked at the peak of the trick. Overcorrecting, he *did* lose his balance. He face-planted in the lake, rocking the pontoon boat with the splash.

"Down," called Cameron, who was spotting.

"I'll say," agreed my brother.

Adam, who was driving now, brought the boat around. When he cut the motor and the Nickelback, he, Cameron and McGillicuddy hooted and clapped for Sean almost as hard as they'd clapped for me. I wished they would quit. I didn't want Sean mad. Flirting with him was turning out to be a lot harder than I'd thought.

Sean grinned at them from the water. Even though his turn hadn't been very long, clearly he'd had enough. He took off his life vest and tossed it up into the boat. Then he disappeared under the surface.

"What's he doing?" I asked, leaning over the side of the boat, searching for him beneath the water. If the tow rope had gotten tangled, he might need help. And *someone* would need to go in the water with him, perhaps accidentally sliding against him down where no one else could see.

"Boo!" A handful of bryozoa rushed up at me from the lake.

I screamed (for once I didn't have to think about this girl-reaction) and fell backward into the boat. Sean hefted himself over the side with one arm, holding the bryozoa high in the other hand. It dripped green slime through his fingers. "Bwa-ha-ha!" He came after me.

I squealed again. It was so unbelievably fantastic that he was flirting with me, but bryozoa was involved. Was it worth it? No. I paused on the side of the boat, ready to jump back into the water myself. He might chase me around the lake with the bryozoa, but at least it would be diluted. On second thought, I didn't particularly want to jump into the very waters the bryozoa had come from.

Sean solved the problem for me. He slipped behind me and showed me he was holding the ties of my bikini in his free hand. If I jumped, Sean would take possession of my bikini top.

I had *thought* about double knotting my bikini. I'd hoped against hope that Stage

Two: Bikini would work, and that Sean might try something like this. Of course, I didn't *really* want my top to come off in front of everyone. Nay, in front of *anyone*. But I'd checked the double knots in the mirror. They'd looked . . . well, double knotted, for protection, sort of like wearing a turtleneck to the prom. I'd re-tied the strings normally.

Now I wished I'd double knotted after all. Sean brought the dripping slime close to my shoulder. "Go ahead and jump," he said, twisting my bikini ties in his fingers.

"Sean," came McGillicuddy's voice in warning. This surprised me. My brother had never taken up for me before. Of course, none of the boys had ever crossed this particular line.

But that was nothing compared with my surprise when the bryozoa suddenly lobbed out of Sean's hand, sailed through the air, and plopped into the lake. Adam, standing behind him, must have shoved his arm.

Which meant I owed Adam my gratitude for saving me. Except I didn't *want* him to save me from Sean, and I thought I'd made that clear. Saving me from Sean with *bryozoa* . . . that was a more iffy proposition. I wasn't sure whether I should give Adam the *little dolphin* look again when our eyes met. But it didn't matter. When I turned around, he was already stepping over Cameron's legs to return to the driver's seat.

Sean was watching me, though. And Sean wiped the bryozoa residue from his hand across my stomach. This was the third time a boy had ever touched my bare tummy, and I'd had enough.

Through gritted teeth, like any extra movement might spread the bryozoa further across my skin, I told him, "I like you less than I did." I bailed over the side of the boat—the side opposite where the bryozoa had returned to its native habitat. Deep in the warm water, I scrubbed at my tummy with both hands. A combination of bryozoa waste and Sean germs: it was the best of times, it was the worst of times. Leaning toward worst, because now I had slime on my hands. Or maybe this was psychosomatic. Holding my hands open in front of me in the water, I didn't *see* any slime. I rubbed my hands together anyway.

Something dove into the water beside me in a rush of bubbles. I came up for air.

Sean surfaced, too, tossing sparkling drops of water from his hair. "You still like me a lot, though, right?"

"No prob. Green is the new black." Giving up on getting clean, I swam a few strokes back toward the platform to get out again. What I needed was a shower with chlorinated water and disinfectant soap. I might need to bubble out my belly button with hydrogen peroxide.

"What if I made it up to you?" He splashed close behind me. "What if I helped you get clean? We don't want you dirty." He moved both hands around me under the water, and up and down across my tummy.

It was the *fourth* time a boy had touched my tummy! And it was very awkward. He bobbed so close behind me that I had a hard time treading water without kicking him. I needed to choose between flirting and breathing.

Cameron and my brother leaned over the side of the boat and gaped at us, which didn't help matters. I'd been afraid of this. Flirting with Sean was no fun if the other boys acted like we were lepers. Well, okay, it *was* fun, but not as fun as it was supposed to be.

Obviously I would need to give McGillicuddy the *little dolphin* talk. I wasn't sure I could do this with Cameron—Cameron and I didn't have heart-to-heart convos—but I might need to make an exception, if he continued to watch us like we were a dirty movie on Pay-Per-View (which I'd *also* seen a lot of. Life with boys).

BEEEEEEEEEEEEEEEE—

Sean and I started and turned toward the boat. Still behind the steering wheel, Adam had his chin in his hand and his elbow on the horn.

—EEEEEEEEEEEEEEEEEEEEEEEEE

Damn it! I turned around to face Sean and gave him a wry smile, but he'd already taken his hands away from my tummy. The horn really ruined the mood.

—EEEEEEEEEEEEEEEEEEEEEEEE

Sean hauled himself up onto the platform. I followed close behind him, and (glee!) he put out a hand to help me. Cameron and my brother yelled at Adam.

—EEEEEEEEEEEEEEEEEEEEEEEEP.

"Oh!" Adam said as if he'd had no idea he'd been laying on the horn. He looked at his elbow like it belonged to someone else.

I was in the boat with Sean now, and he

was still holding my hand. Or, maybe I was still *clinging* to his hand, but this is a question of semantics. In any case, I pulled him by the hand past the other boys to the bow. We didn't have privacy. There was no privacy on a wakeboarding boat. At least we had the boat's windshield between us and the others.

As I turned to sit down on the bench, I stuck out my tongue at Adam behind the windshield. He crossed his eyes at me.

Sean sat very close to me again. He pretended to yawn and stretch, then settled his arm around my shoulders. I smiled at him and tried to think of something to say. After years of him being vaguely pleasant to me but basically ignoring me, it had never occurred to me that we had nothing in common but wakeboarding—and I suspected wakeboarding might be a touchy subject right now. We didn't need to talk. He kept his arm around me for the short ride back to the marina.

Instead of driving straight to the wharf where we usually parked the boat, Adam slowed at the marina dock so the boys could mock Mr. Vader, who hadn't moved from the position he'd been in when I splashed him, except he'd started on another beer. The boys told him he was all washed up and he should enter a wet T-shirt contest with that figure, and so forth. My brother called to Dad, "Nice save, Pops."

"Hey." Dad tipped his beer to us. "You've got to be fast with Lori around."

"I have to say, young lady," grumbled Mr. Vader. "I was very impressed with all your shenanigans. Right up to the point I got doused. I want you to plan to close the Crappie Festival show until further notice."

Which meant, *Until you screw up*. That was okay. He'd told me I was better than the boys at something for once in my life! I turned to Sean and beamed so big that my cheeks hurt.

Sean squinted into the sun, wearing that strange, fixed smile. Even my brother and Cameron gave each other puzzled looks rather than congratulating me again. Only Adam met my eyes. He shook his head at me.

Oh, crap. Crappy. Holy Crappie Festival! I had upset the natural order. After Adam had already upset the natural order in team calisthenics. I should have thought *all* of this through better.

Sean began, "But I didn't even get a chance to—"

"I saw what happened," Mr. Vader told him. "You had your chance. The Big Kahuna has spoken."

"Race you to the wharf," Adam called. Mr. Vader said something to my dad, put down his beer, and tried to hurl himself up the steps to the marina faster than Adam idled the boat. The boys were doofuses, and it was genetic. Adam let Mr. Vader win by half a length, touching the bow of the boat to the padded edge of the wharf just after Mr. Vader dashed past. The boys howled, and someone threw a couple of dollar bills at Mr. Vader. He picked up each bill like it mattered and limped back down the stairs toward my dad.

Then Sean jumped out of the bow to tie up the boat. He, Cameron, and my brother tried to trip each other as they took armfuls of equipment into the warehouse with them. No one gave me a single backward glance.

Adam cut the engine. "Now you've screwed up."

"How?" I asked casually, stepping out of the boat. "You think Sean won't want to go out with me now that I've taken his spot in the show?"

Adam just looked at me. That's *exactly* what he thought. I was getting tired of his warnings about Sean. I gathered my clothes and my backpack, turned on my heel, and flounced away. Which was fairly ineffective with bare feet, on a rough concrete wharf.

"You'll see at the party tonight," Adam called after me.

"No, *you'll* see," I threw over my shoulder. Sean and his pride would prove no match for Stage Three: Slinky Cleavage-Revealing Top.

Five

As I walked home, balancing on the seawall that kept the Vaders' yard and my yard from falling into the lake, my cell phone rang. I pulled it out of my backpack without hurrying. The only people who ever called me were my dad, my brother, assorted Vaders to tell me to come early or late to work (including Sean, but he always sounded grumpy that he had to call me, so it wasn't as big a thrill as you'd think), Tammy to tell me to come early or late to tennis practice, and Frances. I glanced at the caller ID screen and clicked the phone on. "What's up, Fanny?"

From the time Mom died until I was eleven, Frances the au pair had hung out in the background of my life. Once Sean overheard someone calling her Fanny, which apparently is a nickname for Frances. We found this shocking. I mean, who has a nickname that's a synonym for derrière? Who's named Frances in the first place? So the boys started calling her Fanny the Nanny. Then, Booty the Babysitter. Then, Butt I Don't Need a Governess. This had everything to do with the nickname Fanny and the fact that she tried not to get upset at being addressed in this undignified manner when she was trying to raise compassionate, responsible children. It had nothing to do with her having an outsized rumpus. Frances had a cute figure, if you could see it under all that hippie-wear.

"I'm on the dock," she said.

I peered the half-mile across the lake and waved to her. I could hardly make her out at that distance, against the trees that sheltered the Harbargers' house, where she nannied now. I could only see her homemade purple patchwork dress, which was probably visible from Mars.

"The children and I watched the last part of your wakeboarding run," she said. "You've improved so much since last year!"

"Thanks! But that's not why you called. You're dying to know what happened with Sean."

Frances was in on my Life Makeover. Not the fashion part—sheesh, look at her. She hadn't even given me advice on what to do. I wandered into the Harbargers' house every week or so and told her how my plan was shaping up, and she told me I was being ridiculous and it would never work. I guess I went to her because I wanted to hear some motherly input. We had the perfect relationship. She wasn't really my mother, so I could listen to her input and then do the opposite. The difference between me and girls with mothers was that I didn't get in trouble for this.

"Let me guess," she said. "When Sean saw you in a bikini, he acted incrementally more cozy to you. Therefore you expected him to profess his love. You honestly did. And he didn't do a thing."

"Rrrrrnt!" I made the game-show noise for a wrong answer. I told her what had really happened.

"What?" she said when I told her Adam beat Sean at calisthenics. "What?" she said when I told her I landed the air raley. "What?"

she said when I told her Sean wiped out. As I got to the part about Sean touching my tummy *repeatedly*, she interrupted me so often that I had to pitch a frustrated fit. I threw the phone down to the grass, cupped my hands around my mouth, and hollered across the lake, "LET. ME. FINISH!" *Inish, inish, inish,* said my echo. I picked up the phone and told her the rest of the story, ending with my plan to implement Stage Three that night.

"But you don't really think wearing a low-cut top to the boys' party will solve all your problems, do you?" she asked.

"Of course not. I think wearing a low-cut top to the boys' party will show Sean I'm ready for him."

"Lori, no girl is ever ready for a boy like Sean. How were finals?" Clearly she wanted to change the subject to impress upon me that boys were not all there was to a teenage girl's life. As if.

"Finals?" I asked.

"Yes, finals. To graduate from the tenth grade? You took them yesterday."

Wow, it was hard to believe I'd played hopscotch with the quadratic equation only twenty-seven hours ago. Thinking back, it seemed like I'd sleepwalked through the past nine months of school, compared with everything that had happened today.

Time flew when you were having Sean.

Mr. Vader let the boys throw a party at their house every Friday night during the summers. He reasoned that if they were home, they weren't out drag racing the pink truck against Mrs. Vader's Volvo. So I'd been to a million of these parties. It should have been old hat. Yet it was new hat. I had put on my seductress bonnet. Ha! Not really. This would have dented my hair, which I'd blown out long, straight and bryozoa-free.

We'd had a lot of rain in May, which made the lake full, the grass lush, the trees happy, and the ground soft. Walking through my yard into the boys' yard in high heels was like wading in the lake where the sand was deep, feet sinking with every step. I felt like Elizabeth Bennet in *Pride and Prejudice* (tenth grade English) hiking through pastures to a house party, her petticoat six inches deep in mud. Wait a minute—oh crap, I'd forgotten my petticoat.

And what ho, cheerio, here was Mr. Darcy getting his groove on with Miss

Bingley under a massive oak tree. Actually it was only Adam and Rachel.

I did a double take. Adam pressed Rachel against the tree, kissing her. Deeply.

This shouldn't have surprised me. They'd been together for a month. He was my age, and she was a year younger, so neither of them had a driver's license. But they met at the arcade or the bowling alley. I'd even seen them kiss before, a quick peck. I'd just never seen them kiss like *this*.

Knowing Adam, I would have thought his love life would be like every other part of his life: dangerous. It started that way. Since middle school, he'd followed in Sean's footsteps, coming on to a different girl every week. I had imagined this would continue as Adam got older. The only difference between Adam and Sean would be that Adam would get in a lot of fist fights with the girls' exboyfriends in the movie theater parking lot, and occasionally I would hear a rumor about a drive-by that he would swear wasn't true.

Instead, he'd been with Rachel for a month. A whole month. It seemed stable. Even boring. Well! Maybe her own budding womanhood had brought out the pirate in him. Yaaarg.

He broke the kiss, turned, and stared at me as if I had no right to watch what was going on in a public place. That's when I realized *I* was staring at *them*. Standing still in the middle of the yard, just staring, my heels settling in the dirt. Watching him kiss Rachel bothered me, but I couldn't put my finger on why. There was nothing to do but wade to the front porch of his house.

I rang the doorbell.

Nothing happened.

After a few minutes, I pressed my ear to the door and rang the doorbell again. I definitely heard the chime of the doorbell inside, the bass beat from the stereo, and laughter. Why didn't someone come to the door? Maybe they had a closed-circuit camera on me right now and everybody at the party was watching me on TV, taking bets on how long I'd stand there before wading home. I peered into the top corners of the porch for a camera.

Why hadn't I dispensed with the last three coats of eye shadow and gone with my brother to the party when he told me he was leaving the house, like usual? He was a dork, but at least he was totally comfortable in social situations, like Dad. Comfortable, or oblivious, which amounted to the same thing.

The door swung open, revealing Ashton Kutcher. Just kidding! It was actually my tennis team captain, Tammy.

"Tammeeeee!" I squealed, hugging her. This was what girls did.

"Loreeeee," she said in her husky, low-key voice, playing along. "I figured someone had better open the door, because you obviously weren't going to. Why'd you ring the doorbell? No one's ringing the doorbell. They just walk in. Besides, don't you practically live here?"

Did I? I supposed I knew the territory, and always hoped someone in the house noticed me. This sounded less like I was a member of the family and more like I was a stray dog. I changed the subject. "What are *you* doing here? Are you friends with Sean or Adam or Cameron?"

She knitted her eyebrows at me. "I'm friends with *you*."

"Right!" I said. Was she? I fought the urge to look behind me, like she'd actually been talking to someone over my shoulder the whole time.

"You look great!" she said, pulling me

through the doorway and into the brighter light of the foyer. "Cute top, and your eye shadow looks great!"

"Thanks!" I watched her reaction to make sure she'd said what I'd thought she said. The stereo was loud, and *you look great* was not something I heard every day, or every year.

"You weren't planning to wear mascara?" she asked. "Usually when people wear shadow and liner that heavy, they wear mascara with it."

"I do have some! I forgot! Thank you!" I grabbed her hand. She flinched. I didn't let go. "Will you come with me to my house to make sure I put it on right? I'm serious."

Her eyes moved past me out the door, toward my house. "You live next door, right?" Clearly she didn't want to venture too far from the party with a weird-eyed lunatic such as myself.

"Noooooo," I said sarcastically. "I live on a planet far, far away. Women are from Venus. Come on." I pulled her toward my house until she seemed to be keeping pace with me. Then I dropped her hand. I knew girls pulled each other by the hand and squealed a lot, but it was too weird for me to do it for long.

Adam and Rachel were still making out. They'd moved behind the tree where I wouldn't have seen them unless I'd been looking for them (which I was). I almost pointed them out to Tammy, then decided against it. I didn't want to sound like a fifth grader: *Wow, kissing!*

"You really do look cute," Tammy said, "other than the—you know. Why the makeover?"

I took a deep breath and readied myself for my next step into girldom: spilling a giggly secret. When we'd gotten far enough away from Adam and Rachel that they couldn't hear me, I said, "I have a crush on somebody. I'm trying to get him to notice me."

"Sean Vader?"

I stopped short in my garage, and Tammy ran full force into me. I shoved her and shrieked, "*Why would you think that?*"

"Gee, I don't know," she yelled back. "Maybe because *you have told me this over and over*!"

I blinked. "I have?"

"Maybe not in so many words."

Oh *no*! "So, I've been really obvious at school?" I tried to keep most of the horror from my voice.

"Isn't everyone?" She flipped her hair back over her shoulder with a tennis ace flick of the wrist that I would try later to reproduce (and fail). "Girls fall all over themselves when Sean comes around. He's hot, and soooooo sweet."

"He sounds like fondue." Mmmmm, fondue. I opened the door and led the way into my house.

I didn't think we were being quiet, particularly. High heels may have looked dainty, but they didn't sound that way on a tile floor. Maybe it was just that my dad was so absorbed in the convo on his cell phone. For whatever reason, when we emerged from the kitchen into the den, he started, and he stuffed the phone down by his side in the cushions. I was sorry I'd startled him, but it really was comical to see this big blond manly man jump three feet off the sofa when he saw two teenage girls. I mean, it would have been funny if it weren't so sad.

Dad was a ferocious lawyer in court. Out of court, he was one of those Big Man on Campus types who shook hands with everybody from the mayor to the alleged ax murderer. A lot like Sean, actually. There were only two things Dad was afraid of. First, he wigged out when anything in the house was misplaced. I won't even go into all the arguments we'd had about my room being a mess. They'd ended when I told him it was *my* room, and if he didn't stop bugging me about it, I would put kitchen utensils in the wrong drawers, maybe even *hide* some (cue horror movie music). No spoons for you! Second, he was easily startled, and very pissed off afterward. "Damn it, Lori!" he hollered.

"It's great to see you too, loving father. Lo, I have brought my friend Tammy to witness our domestic bliss. She's on the tennis team with me." Actually, *I* was on the tennis team with *her*.

"Hello, Tammy. It's nice to meet you," Dad said without getting up or shaking her hand or anything else he would normally do. While the two of them recited a few more snippets of polite nonsense, I watched my dad. From the angle of his body, I could tell he was protecting that cell phone behind the cushions.

I nodded toward the hiding place. "Hot date?"

I was totally kidding. I didn't expect him to say, "When?"

So I said, "Ever." And then realized I'd brought up a subject that I didn't want to bring up, especially not while I was busy being self-absorbed. I clapped my hands. "Okay, then! Tammy and I are going upstairs very loudly, and after a few minutes we will come back down, ringing a cowbell. Please continue with your top secret phone convo."

I turned and headed for the stairs. Tammy followed me. I thought Dad might order me back, send Tammy out, and give me one of those lectures about my attitude (who, me?). But obviously he was chatting with Pamela Anderson and couldn't *wait* for me to leave the room. Behind us, I heard him say, "I'm so sorry. I'm still here. Lori came in. Oh, yeah? I'd like to see you try."

"He seems jumpy," Tammy whispered on the stairs.

"Always," I said.

"Do you have a lot of explosions around your house?"

I glanced at my watch. "Not this early." I passed through my bedroom, into my bathroom, and found the mascara in the drawer. Poised with wand to eye, I realized Tammy hadn't followed me. I leaned through the bathroom doorway.

She stood in the middle of my bedroom, gazing around with wide eyes. I hadn't made my bed. In three years. And the walls were plastered with wakeboarding posters and snowboarding posters and surfing posters (I was going to learn to snowboard and surf someday, too). It all might have been overwhelming at first—not exactly *House Beautiful*.

"Is this McGillicuddy's room?" she asked.

"What! No. McGillicuddy's a neat freak. Also he collects Madame Alexander dolls."

She turned her wide eyes on me.

"Kidding! I'm kidding," I backtracked. Why did I have to make up stuff like that? My family was weird enough for real.

She stepped over to my bookshelf to peer at the stacks of wakeboarding mags and sci-fi novels. Well, let her stare, the bi-yotch. I didn't need her damn help. I swiped the mascara across my lashes and popped back out of the bathroom. "Ready?"

She looked up at me guiltily like she'd gotten caught thumbing through my issues of *Playboy* (stolen from McGillicuddy, and more useful for learning what not to wear than teen fashion mags). But she hadn't found those yet. Standing at my bedside table, she held the photo of my mother.

She set the photo down and narrowed her eyes at me. "*You're* not ready." She came into the bathroom and explained the aesthetic we were going for was not clumps of lashes honed to points and sticking out from my eyeballs like the tentacles of a starfish. Somehow in the purchase of my fine cosmetics, I'd missed out on the idea of an eyelash comb. She used a regular hair comb to tease my lashes apart.

We stomped back down the stairs (no cowbell, but I made air-raid siren noises to warn my dad) and waded across the yard. Adam and Rachel were *still* making out behind the tree, like they hadn't seen each other for a year. Jeez, we'd just gotten out of school *yesterday*.

I tried to look without really looking and letting on to Tammy I was looking. Both Adam's hands were on Rachel's shoulders, holding her in place while he kissed her. Both *her* hands were under his T-shirt, on his stomach—his stomach hard with muscle, his smooth tanned skin . . . I couldn't see this, of course, but I knew it was there.

It had never occurred to me to be jealous of Rachel before. Suddenly I was burning with jealousy, sweating in the humid night. It must be that I saw Rachel as an understudy for Holly and Beige and all the girls at my school who knew what to wear and how to act or, if they didn't, hid it well. I could totally see a third-grade girl feeling inferior to Rachel and wanting to be Rachel when she grew up. That third-grade girl was thinking someday maybe *she* could have a boyfriend like Adam, who loved her like Adam—

"Argh!" I bellowed as I pitched face-first onto the pine needles. I must have gotten my heel caught in a snake hole.

"Are you okay?" Tammy asked, holding out a hand to help me up. "Nice trick. You should put that in your wakeboarding routine."

"What? And steal Adam's thunder?" I brushed myself off. Did I need to go home and change? I was new to this idea of a "wardrobe," and my supply of Slinky Cleavage-Revealing Tops was limited. Fortunately, my denim miniskirt was made to look dirty. It was very me. And the wild pattern in my top probably concealed any decayed-leaf stains. Satisfied, I walked on with Tammy. I didn't look back to see whether Adam had watched me fall. I hadn't forgotten that stare of his.

"Want to play tennis tomorrow night, after it's cooled off a little?" she asked.

"Sure," I said before I thought. Tammy and I played tennis all the time in school. Why not out of school, too? After I'd answered, I realized that of course Sean would ask me out for tomorrow night and I wouldn't get to go with him! Right. I wasn't lucky enough to have problems like that. Silly me. "You shouldn't have to drive all the way down here to pick me up and then drive me all the way back."

"I don't mind."

Stepping onto the Vaders' porch, I said, "McGillicuddy can come get me when we're through." My brother never had anything to do on Saturday night. It ran in the family.

"McGillicuddy?" she asked.

We walked back into the party. Fluttering my finely separated lashes, I could hardly believe my luck. Usually at parties I wandered in alone and hoped someone took pity and talked to me. Then, by degrees, I faded into the shadows. Tonight I was entering the party *with* someone.

Of course, the instant we hit the wall of crowd and sound, she pointed across the dark room and shouted above the music, "I'd completely forgotten McGillicuddy was coming back from college! I'm going to say hi." The two people I felt most comfortable hanging with, hanging with each other instead!

Except for the kids from Birmingham and Montgomery who were vacationing on the lake with their parents and had wandered into the party, I knew all these people from school. I'd been in school with most of them since kindergarten. For some reason, this didn't help, and possibly made things worse. I watched Tammy weave between knots of people to hug McGillicuddy. I thought about going after her. But then I might look like I didn't want her to leave me by myself because I wasn't good at talking to people at parties. Imagine!

Suddenly things looked way, way up. I saw Sean in the darkness, next to the stairs, with his back to me. He stood a few inches taller than his friends who'd just graduated too, who surrounded him. Sean was always surrounded.

As I crossed the room to him, folks kept stepping in my way, wanting to say hey and have conversations with me, of all things. The one time I *wasn't* interested in being well-liked. Drat! I made nicey-nicey, go away, and resumed my uphill trek across the room, only to have someone else stop me.

By the time I finally reached him, my heart pounded. But it was now or never. I made myself grin at his friends as I slid my hand across his T-shirt, feeling his hard stomach underneath the cotton. I almost flinched at how good and how intimate it felt, but through the marvel of my own willpower, I did not flinch. I laid my head playfully against his chest, as I'd seen girls do when they claimed to be just friends with a guy but everyone whispered something more was going on.

I half-expected him to shout, "Get off me!" and shove me away. Not because Sean would ever do this to a girl—he had more charming ways of extricating himself from cretins—but because my life generally had been a long series of mortifications, and Sean shouting in alarm at my embrace would fit right in. The other half of me expected him to chuckle gently, but not make a move of his own quite yet. It might take him a while to get used to the new me.

He didn't chuckle. He didn't shove me away. He did *exactly* what he was supposed to. He slipped his arm around my waist and drew me closer against his warm body. I felt him nodding at something one of the other guys said about baseball, but he didn't say a word to me or anyone. As if a greeting like this from me were the most natural thing in the world. He smelled even better than usual, too, just a hint of cologne. A woodsy scent with undertones of musk and gun-powder.

I snuggled against him, nose close to his warm, scented chest, and enjoyed a few more seconds of this tingling paradise. What heaven if my whole summer could be like this—

His low voice vibrating through my body, he asked his friends, "Have you been watching the Braves? Tim Hudson or what?"

Oh God, I was hugging *Adam*!

Six

I jerked away from him. Almost instantly I realized I shouldn't jerk away from him, because the situation would be slightly less mortifying if I pretended I'd known it was Adam all along.

The damage was done. Worse, I didn't have a chance to burst out the front door and run—not walk, *run*—all the way home, dash upstairs to the computer in my room, and book a one-way ticket to Antarctica, to join the commune there for teenagers too socially challenged for the chess club. Before I could take another step away, he caught my elbow.

"Later," he called over his shoulder to the guys. He pulled me into a corner and bent down to whisper in my ear, "You're blushing."

I opened my lips. I didn't seem to be taking in enough oxygen through my nose. "I'm sunburned," I breathed.

"You thought I was Sean." The little dolphin was smiling, enjoying my discomfort too much for my taste.

"No, I didn't." I made an effort to slow down my breathing through nose *or* mouth. My bosom was heaving, I tell you. I had a heaving bosom!

And Adam noticed. He focused on the V of the Slinky Cleavage-Revealing Top Meant for Another, and slowly, slowly dragged his light blue eyes up to meet my eyes. "I should have said something. I didn't realize what was happening at first. And then, when I did, I was *really* enjoying myself."

"Shut up. I didn't think you were Sean."

"You thought I was Sean, because I'm as big as him." He winked at me.

There was no mistaking him for Sean now that I was staring up at him. I tried to figure out what had fooled me into assuming it was him without checking his face and the length of his hair. It could have been his height compared with the boys two years older than him. But something else was different about Adam. He was more confident. More relaxed. More tingle-worthy, like Sean had always been. Those friendly prickles spread across my chest again as Adam's fingers moved a little, reminding me he still held my elbow.

I pulled reluctantly out of his grip. "It's not funny, Adam. What if somebody tells Rachel?"

"She won't mind. She knows we're friends."

From my end, the hug hadn't felt like we were friends. It had felt like we were teetering on the very edge of friendship, about to tumble down a waterfall into depths unknown. With rocks hidden underneath the water. Hard ones.

Or *I* was about to take a tumble, by myself. *He* still stood in his living room like always, at the edge of his crowded party, laughing down at me, thinking, *The Slinky Cleavage-Revealing Top has cut off the blood supply to Lori McGillicuddy's brain.*

I reached up to his neck. Surprise finally flashed in his eyes—ha!—but he let me pull the skull-and-crossbones pendant on the leather string out from under his shirt.

"You make sure this shows at all times," I said. "It's your cowbell. It tells me when you're coming." I patted his chest, which I should not have done if we really were just friends. As we've established, my brain was walking a few steps behind my body and couldn't quite catch up. Face still burning, I took a few steps into the crowd. Where would Sean most likely be? Flirting with Holly and Beige simultaneously, pitting the best friends against each other to see what would happen. But no, they were dancing together at the edge of the crowd in the living room, without Sean.

I stopped suddenly.

Walked back to Adam, who was still watching me.

"What's wrong?" he asked.

"You're right," I breathed, my words sinking into the pit of my stomach. "Rachel won't mind us hugging."

"What do you mean?"

"She's in the side yard, making out with Sean."

By the time I'd kicked off my (dirty) heels and dashed after Adam outside, he'd already gotten himself pinned flat on his back under Sean on the pine needles. I winced as Sean shifted to get better leverage and pressed his forearm harder across Adam's neck.

"Sean!" I hollered, running all the way around them, trying to find a way in. Sometimes I couldn't pull Sean off Adam, or I even got hit myself. There was a time when I would have tried anyway, disregarding my personal safety. This was back when we were all very small and made of rubber. Nowadays, hollering was more effective, unless they were really into it, in which case nothing would work.

They were really into it. Adam managed to kick Sean off him and get in a blow to Sean's chin. Usually they didn't hit each other in the face because Mrs. Vader would see the bruises and they'd get in trouble. Adam must be angry enough tonight not to care.

Sean came right back with a punch to Adam's gut. While Adam was absorbing that one, Sean pinned Adam's arm high behind him, tripped him, forced him to the ground, and put one knee on his back. Tonight Sean was more aggressive than usual, intent on causing more pain.

Or—Something wasn't right. Had they switched shirts? Surely not. Sean didn't let Adam borrow his clothes. Slowly it dawned on me that Sean was Adam and Adam was Sean. For the first time ever, Adam was kicking Sean's ass.

"Holy shit," I said helpfully. "Adam, let him go."

Adam looked up at me, blue eyes shadowed in the dark between the trees, skull and crossbones swinging at his neck.

This gave Sean the opportunity to buck Adam off. He snatched Adam down to the ground and punched him.

"Sean," I said, stepping close over them again. They weren't listening to me. I looked over at Rachel, who had her hands over her mouth and her toes turned in. She looked exactly like a James Bond girl from the pre-Halle Berry era, one of those ditzes who stood safely in the corner and *never* had a dagger when she needed one, like Honey Ryder, or Plenty O'Toole. "Rachel, a little help?" I called.

She stared at me with big doe eyes like she had *no idea* what I was talking about. She'd been with Adam for a month and she'd never seen one of his fights with Sean?

"Call Adam off!" I yelled at her. "Or Sean. Whichever one you can get!" Both.

"Sean, stop," she said in a whiny little voice that couldn't have reprimanded a Chihuahua.

"Forget it." I knelt down on the pine needles and shouted directly at Sean and Adam, on their level. "I'll go get your dad. Your dad will come down into your party and cuss at you and spit on the ground in front of your friends."

They didn't even slow down. Whoever was on top had the other in a choke hold so real, the victim was turning red.

"I'll go get your mom!"

Adam gave Sean a final shake and stood up quickly, before Sean could catch his leg and pull him down. "What is the *matter* with you?" Adam screamed.

Yeah. What was the *matter* with Sean? He was making out with Rachel, that's what. This was terrible! It blew my theory out of the water that Sean had never asked me out because I was too young for him. Rachel was a year younger than *me*!

Normally I would have given up, slunk home, and broken out the Cheetos. I would have immersed myself in *I, Robot* for comfort (again) and put it down after every paragraph to wallow in my own outrage and loss. He'd flirted with *me* just that afternoon! He'd wiped bryozoa on *me*!

Luckily, this was no normal night. Tonight I was on a mission. So I reasoned that all wasn't lost. Maybe Sean had flirted with me because he was overcome by my charms and wit (ho ho), but he didn't see me as the girlfriend type. After all, I'd never been anyone's girlfriend. Rachel didn't have this problem. Sean had watched Rachel go out with Adam for a month.

Sean stood up more slowly than Adam had, taking deep, ragged breaths, clearly hurting. I waited for Adam to decide Sean had had enough of his wrath for now, and turn to Rachel. I looked forward to hearing what Adam would call her, to save me the trouble. But he never even glanced in her direction. He said again, still to Sean, "What the hell is the matter with you?" His voice broke.

Now Cameron and McGillicuddy came jogging through the trees, with Tammy behind them, and more interested spectators from the party bringing up the rear. Even though the fight was over, McGillicuddy stepped between Sean and Adam. A smart move, because these things had been known to flare up again. Which was exactly what the ring of spectators hoped for. Tammy tried to catch my eye. I shook my head.

Cameron took Adam's face in both hands and peered at the big smudge under his eye. He let Adam go and hissed at me, "Get rid of him in case Mom comes down."

I felt honored to be included in the intrigue. But why couldn't Cameron ask me to get rid of Sean instead?

That was okay, for now. Adam needed me. I put my hand on his back and said, "Walk away." We moved through the yard, toward the side of the house. A pine needle hung from one of his brown curls in the back.

After fifteen paces, his breathing had slowed almost to normal. I felt him start to turn. "Don't look back," I said.

He took a deep, calming breath through his nose. He was fighting the part of ADD that made him short-tempered and impulsive. The part that made him attempt to smash his big brother's face in.

"Try not to take it so seriously," I said in what I hoped was a soothing tone. Which was hard for me. Generally I was about as soothing as body lotion with skin conditioners and ground glass, but this was important. "It's probably a temporary thing. He's mad at you for making the size jokes this afternoon—"

"I didn't start the size jokes!"

"You finished the size jokes. So he seduced your girlfriend. She said yes because you've been together for a whole month. Maybe things have gotten into a rut." We passed the corner of the house and reached the side yard, where no one lingering in the front yard could see us. I stopped him under the floodlight hanging from the eaves. "Let me look at your eye." I reached up to cup his face in my hands, like Cameron had.

"Is my mom going to notice?"

Yes, I thought. "I can't tell," I said. I didn't want him dashing after Sean to get revenge. "Maybe if we cleaned it up."

He pulled off his T-shirt, wet the edge of it with the faucet attached to the house, and brought it to me.

"Sit down," I said. "I can hardly see you way up there."

We sat in the grass. I leaned close, tilted his face to the light, and wiped at the half-dried blood. He watched me with serious eyes.

And I felt that tingle again. The same pesky tingle I'd felt when I hugged him in the living room, when I thought he was Sean. Only I *knew* now he wasn't Sean. And I'd seen Adam without his shirt a million times, including hours of no-shirt goodness that very afternoon. The tingle stayed.

This was only natural, I guessed. We both were still pumped full of adrenalin. We were excited about the fight and mad about Sean and Rachel, and jealous. I was leaning close to him, our lips almost touching. He still smelled like cologne, plus something sexier.

"Well?" His voice broke again. He cleared his throat and said in his deep boy-voice, "Well?"

"Well, it's not coming off." I gave the oozing blood one last gentle wipe and sat back on my heels. "I'm sorry about what happened."

He shrugged and kept giving me that intense, serious look. And I kept tingling. It was almost like he was sending me his adrenalin telepathically, and I could feel was he was feeling.

Which didn't make sense. Because he

ought to be heartbroken about Rachel. But this felt *good*.

"The fireworks are starting without you." I stood up quickly and held out my hand to help him up (for show only—he weighed twice as much as me). He put his shirt back on. Pity. Keeping my hand on his back, I steered him toward the muffled noise of explosions, down through the shadowy backyard to the dock.

Boys—mostly football players my age or a year older—lit bottle rockets and held them until the fuse sparked almost down to their fingers. At the last possible second, they tossed them into the black lake. A pause. Then deep under the surface, the water glowed bright green for an instant. The lake said *foop*.

Adam would probably ask me to help him collect the bottle rocket sticks off the lake bottom tomorrow, another one of his dad's rules. I didn't want to do this, because I'd had an unpleasant bryozoa scare climbing up the ladder of their dock last year. But I preferred the boys shooting bottle rockets into the lake to shooting them toward my yard, which tended to give my dad a nervous breakdown. And I couldn't ask them to stop altogether. Adam got testy if he went more than a few weeks without setting something on fire.

The boys shouted greetings to Adam and shared their bottle rockets with him. He watched the sparks with delight and hardly a hint of evil. Then he handed me a bottle rocket and lit it for me with a lighter from his pocket. I finally relaxed. We forgot all about Rachel and Sean.

For a little while.

Seven

During the school year, Holly and Beige had said micro-miniskirts should be the official tennis team uniform because we could move better during games, and material wouldn't get bunched between our legs like it did with shorts. I'd never had the material-bunching problem myself. I figured Holly and Beige made this up so they'd have an excuse to wear micro-miniskirts to class when we had a tennis meet right after school. Thank God they'd graduated and I was (mostly) rid of them. For me, tennis and fashion didn't mix. Serena Williams I was not.

Normally I would have worn gym shorts and one of Adam's huge T-shirts to play tennis with Tammy. However, the tennis courts sat between the high school and the main road through town, which also ran past the movie theater, the arcade, and the bowling alley. If Sean was out with Rachel, he would drive right by. So it was the official tennis team micro-miniskirt for me.

"Is that part of your makeover to catch Sean? Wearing that skirt when you're not forced to?" Tammy asked as we passed each other, changing ends of the court. We were the only idiots playing tennis on a ninety-degree Saturday night, so we had the court to ourselves. Besides the ball bouncing and the rackets whacking, the only sounds were the cars swishing by on the road and the buzz of floodlights overhead. Still, the echo off the asphalt court made it hard for us to hear each other while we played. So we'd been carrying on a conversation like this for an hour, one sentence every two games when we traded sides.

She beat me twice, and we passed at the net again. "I'll admit it's not much," I said. "I need a new plan, also referred to as The Back-Up Plan When Stage Three: Cleavage Has No Effect on Cradle Robbers. Any advice?"

I won one game, and then she beat me again. As we approached the net, she suggested, "Make him jealous? I don't know. I'm no good at being sneaky and going behind people's backs."

I dropped my racket with a clatter on the court. "Don't look now"—which of course was her cue to look—"but maybe my old plan worked after all! Sean dumped Rachel already, and the pink truck is coming for me!"

The pink truck was an enormous pickup that used to belong to the marina, so old that the red paint had faded to pink and the VADER'S MARINA signs had peeled off the sides. Cameron had taken possession of the pink truck when he turned sixteen. We gave him no end of hell about it. Then, when he graduated from high school, his parents gave him a new truck to take to college, and Sean had inherited the pink truck.

Sean, being Sean, had managed to make the pink truck seem cool. There were many rumors around school about the adventures of Sean in the pink truck with Holly or Beige. I had dreamed of my own adventures in the pink truck. Now my dreams had come true!

Except that in my dreams, I was not a dork. "Sean came to pick me up!" I groaned. "This is terrible! What do I do?"

"Act casual," Tammy said in a level tone, watching the truck park just outside the high chain-link fence. "Interested, but not manic."

"How do I do that? I don't know how to do that!"

"Go hug him hello."

Just then a breeze kissed the back of my neck under my ponytail, reminding me how hot the night was, and how heavily I'd exerted myself chasing Tammy's serves. "I'm sweaty."

"If he likes you, he won't mind." She led the way through the gate and headed for McGillicuddy's side of the truck to distract him for me.

As I walked toward Sean's side, Sean opened the door and started to get out. I had to walk all the way around the big, heavy door to hug— *"Adam!"*

He looked down at me, arms open wide for me because I'd been holding mine out. He dropped his arms when he saw the look on my face. "Nice to see you, too," he said grumpily.

I patted him lightly on one cheek—the cheek opposite the one with the blue bruise under his eye. The pats got harder until I was pretty much slapping him. "Why can't you be Sean? Oh, God." I knew almost before I'd gotten the words out that Adam didn't deserve that. I stood on my tiptoes and slid my arms around him. "I'm so sorry. I didn't mean it."

He didn't say anything. But he did put his arms around my waist.

I looked up at him. "It's just. . . . Why are you driving Sean's truck?"

"It's *my* truck."

Sean must have gotten a new truck for graduation, just like Cameron. And now Adam was driving the pink truck, because—crap. "Oh, Adam, I forgot your sixteenth birthday!"

"I know."

Those two words told me he'd already thought everything I was thinking. Our birthdays were three weeks apart. We'd had a few birthday parties *together* when we were little. How could I have forgotten his freaking birthday? "I was preoccupied with finals," I gasped, "and summer coming up, and—"

"Sean. I know."

"Oh, I'm so sorry," I said sincerely. I hugged him as hard as I could, then started to pull back.

His hands didn't leave my waist. "I'm still kind of mad," he said.

Laughing, I tightened my hold on him. I felt him bend down and put his chin on my shoulder.

On the other side of the truck, talking with McGillicuddy, Tammy raised one eyebrow at me.

That's when I had an Idea.

I ran my hand down Adam's side until I found his hand. "Let's talk privately."

He looked down at his hand in mine like he couldn't quite believe this was happening. I couldn't either. "Okay," he told our hands.

I called across the hood of the truck, "Adam and I will be right back. We're going to talk privately."

Tammy and McGillicuddy stared at us, then each other, then us again. Finally I pulled Adam away, swinging his hand like holding hands with him wasn't the weirdest thing ever. We walked down the sidewalk, around the corner of the fence to the side of the tennis courts that faced the road. The very edge of the pool of light from the tennis courts touched us, so we could be seen from the road: very important to the plan.

I backed him against the fence. I didn't shove him or anything, but I'm sure he felt trapped against the chain links because I stood so close to him, and the determined expression on my face was so frightening.

I squeezed his hand. "I still think Sean and Rachel's little fling is fake. Sean's trying to get revenge on you, and Rachel's trying to make you jealous. She wants to heat up your romance for the summer. In two weeks, by the Crappy Festival, it'll be over with Sean, and things will be back to normal." And Sean would be free again. "But you need to up the stakes to keep her interested. To make sure she comes back and never leaves you. To teach her a lesson."

Adam breathed faster. His blue eyes widened as it dawned on him what I was going to suggest. In fact, he looked close to panic. I almost backed down. I'd be pretty embarrassed if he ran screaming away and hitchhiked with someone on the road just to escape from me. But I had to salvage my chance with Sean. I'd never gotten as close to him as I had yesterday afternoon in the lake! So I pressed ahead.

"You and I should pretend to hook up. That'll show Rachel you're not putting up with her bullshit. And it'll show Sean I'm girlfriend material. We'll drive them mad, I tell you, mad!" I made a joke out of it in case Adam burst into uncontrollable laughter at the idea of even pretending to hook up with me. Then I could say I'd been kidding all along. I knew Adam valued me as a friend. But I offered him a way out in case he thought I was a dog.

He swallowed, still watching me, alarmed. "You want to hook up with me. To make Rachel jealous, so I can get her back."

"Right," I said, wondering why this was so hard for him to understand. Maybe he didn't watch as much *Laguna Beach* as I did.

"You think that would work? It would make her jealous to see me with another girl?"

"Sure." It was looking more and more like my dog theory was correct. "Unless you think I'm the wrong girl for the job. I'm just suggesting you do this with me because I'm trying to hook Sean, too." Did he think being with me would ruin his chances with

Rachel or any other girl at our school forever, as surely as if he'd gone out with Godzilla?

"Okay," he said quickly.

"Okay?" I had thought it would be harder to convince him. I'd missed something. Which, I'll admit, was not all that unusual.

"Okay, we'll pretend to hook up." He still watched me. His eyes traveled from my eyes to one of my ears, down my neck and further down to my cleavage (thank you sports bra!). He actually leaned back against the fence for better viewing of my legs beneath the micro-miniskirt. Then he met my gaze again. Like he was surveying what he had to pretend to hook up with, and it checked out, with no damage to his rep.

I should have appreciated this. I passed inspection! But his gaze made me uncomfortable enough that the pesky tingle returned. Worse, he seemed to sense he was causing me to tingle. He made that face with his jaw dropped, trying not to smile. Then he gave up and broke into the broadest grin I'd seen on his face since—well, since yesterday afternoon, when he beat Sean at push-ups.

A memory flashed into my mind of Adam, age eight, jumping off the roof because Sean dared him to. (Broken ankle.)

I wondered what I'd gotten myself into.

Suddenly very nervous, I rubbed my tingling hands together and looked toward the road. "Should we drive to the movie theater parking lot where more people will see us together? We could pretend to k—" I looked back at Adam at that moment, and something stopped me in the way he watched me.

"Iss," he said, nodding.

"And they'll tell everyone. It'll get back to Sean and Rachel."

Now he was shaking his head no. "That's not going to work. We can't stage it so carefully. I'm an awful actor. Something tells me you'll never win an Oscar, either."

"Hey—"

"So we need to make it look natural. We need to act like we're into each other all the time, without checking first to see if someone is watching." His hand was trembling in mine. "Maybe this is the first time we've realized we're into each other. And maybe this is our first kiss."

He leaned down. When his face got

within a few inches of mine, I giggled. Not the fake giggle of a tomboy raised by wolves, either. A real, girly, high-pitched giggle that originated somewhere in my sinuses and made me want to slap myself. There was hope for me yet.

"See?" he whispered against my lips. "This is what we're trying to avoid. We need to act like we *want* to do this." And he kissed me.

There were still a few inches between our bodies. So there was no embrace. Only his lips, soft, warm, on my lips.

Our fingers, interlaced.

A tingle so strong, it turned into a vibration.

A hick driving by on the road, hollering, "Get a room, Vader! Wooooo!"

Adam laughed a little against my lips. I thought I detected the slightest shudder, like he felt the vibration too. Then he backed up and looked at me. "Is that what you wanted?"

"Yes," I breathed. "Is that what *you* wanted?"

His smile faded. "Yeah. Come on." He led me back up the sidewalk, toward Tammy and McGillicuddy still talking together but never taking their eyes off us. When we got close to the truck, Adam asked me, "Will you go out with me tomorrow night?"

"I'd love to," I said, focusing only on him like I had no idea my brother was staring a hole through my head.

"I'll pick you up at seven," Adam said. "No, wait."

"That's fine," I laughed. "You can drive a hundred feet and pick me up at seven."

"I'll walk over at seven." He smiled and twisted a lock of my hair around his finger. "Seven is lucky."

McGillicuddy cleared his throat.

"That's not what I meant!" Adam roared at McGillicuddy in outrage. Adam's cheeks were bright red.

"Are we finished?" Tammy asked quickly. "Lori, didn't you lose four or five balls over the fence in the kudzu?"

McGillicuddy, Adam and I all started for the kudzu patch. But Tammy caught me by the sports bra, and I snapped backward. She waited until the boys were out of earshot before she hissed, "Is there something you want to tell me?"

"Yes!" I said happily. "But you can't tell

anybody. And I don't mean you need to keep this secret the way the tennis team kept a secret last year, by leaking it to the basketball team." I'd seen Holly and Beige work.

"I promise," Tammy said, pulling a tennis ball from her pocket and bouncing it against the truck fender. She'd seen Holly and Beige work, too. On *her* secrets. Personally, I'd never had a secret for them to work on before. I was that popular.

"Don't mention it to McGillicuddy. He might blab it to Cameron, depending on how funny he thought it was. You're the only person I'm telling. So if it gets out, I'll know you spilled it." I explained in brief the ingenious and diabolical plan. "Doesn't that sound ingenious? And diabolical?"

"It sounds hopelessly complicated. Wouldn't it be easier to hook up with Adam for real? He's adorable."

"No, he's not!" I eyed her, unsure I should have shared the diabolical plan with her after all. Granted, Adam *was* adorable. But I was after Sean. I didn't intend to *act* on Adam's adorableness. And at that moment, I realized I didn't want anyone else to act on it, either. He was part of my

Adorable Special Reserve. Now that Tammy was telling me there was indeed a problem with my plan, I found that I didn't want to hear it.

She bounced the ball methodically against the truck. "You think *Sean* is adorable."

"Duh."

"And Adam looks a lot like Sean."

"True dat."

"So why don't you think Adam's adorable?"

I snatched the ball in midair and shook it at her. "Because he's Adam!"

Adam and McGillicuddy had found all the escaped balls. They stood in the kudzu, oblivious to snakes, and threw tennis balls as hard as they could at each other. The balls bounced off their arms and chests, and they dove after the balls into the vines again. Typical. I turned back to Tammy. "You said yourself that Sean was fondue."

"No, *you* said that."

"You said girls fall all over themselves to get to Sean. They don't do that for Adam."

"But wouldn't that be better? You'd have to share Sean. Adam would be yours."

I'd thought girls giggled secrets to each

other because they understood each other. Tammy didn't understand me at *all*.

Adam had made a hangman's noose out of a length of vine and was chasing McGillicuddy down the sidewalk with it. Both of them laughed like ten-year-olds. Adam really did look adorable when he smiled.

So, maybe Tammy was half-right. I knew Adam had been kidding about seven being lucky. I knew he was just playing the part with me, like we'd planned, so he could get Rachel back. But part of me, a tiny part about the size of a candy heart, wished he dreamed about getting lucky with me.

Eight

Sean had the nerve to smile down at me. His blue eyes were lighter than the sky behind him, a spooky blue. He shouted above the drone of the boat motor, "Lori, when we're old enough, I want you to be my girlfriend."

I tried to speak, spluttered, and spit out a lock of my hair the wind had blown into my mouth. I was nothing if not glam. "You're old enough," I told him. "And if Rachel is old enough, *I'm* old enough."

He bent closer and said, "I'll pick you up at seven."

What a thrill! He'd asked me out! I was going out with Sean! Only, those were the words I'd *heard*. What he'd *mouthed* was something different. Like on one of those kung fu movies the boys loved to watch, with English words dubbed over the Chinese sound, and the characters' mouths never quite matching up.

"Bastard!" I sat straight up in my cold, wet bed. I wiped and wiped with my palms, but I could *not* get all my hair out of my mouth. Then I realized what I'd said out loud. "Sorry, Mom," I told her sweet sixteen photo on my bedside table. My alarm clock blared Avril Lavigne, "Keep Holding On."

Right! I vowed to move things along with Sean that day at work. I would make sure he knew I was part of the hot scene. Unfortunately, the instant I stepped into the marina office, I was presented with an obstacle to this goal in the form of a seething matriarch with pinstriped hair.

"Lori!" she roared, spinning around in her office chair.

"Good morning, boss!" I said brightly, giving her a wave.

She narrowed her eyes at me. "It was bad enough when Adam told me yesterday that Sean stole Rachel from him. He wanted me to ground Sean, or take away his Wii."

"Ground him for how long?" If Sean was

grounded, he wouldn't even be able to pick Rachel up and drive her back to his own house. He could only see her if her mom dropped her off. Talk about embarrassing. Sean didn't like to be embarrassed. Instant breakup! On the other hand, if he were grounded for the whole summer, even after he broke up with Rachel, he could never go out with *me*.

"I can't *ground* him," Mrs. Vader squealed. "I can't *ground* a legal adult. And I can't *ground* one son for stealing the other's girlfriend. But I've got to do something. Adam's cheekbone is blue. Sean is holding his jaw at a funny angle and won't let me look at it. The physical fights are bad enough. They can't torture each other psychologically, too!"

Of course they could. They'd been doing it for years. Obviously Sean was careful not to call Adam ADD when their mother was around. Somehow I didn't think pointing this out would help my current situation, so I nodded like I understood her plight. "Do I have gas?"

She folded her arms. "And this morning Adam told me he's going out tonight. With *you*."

"Don't say I didn't warn you," I sang, sweeping my hand down my body in the *all this can be yours* gesture.

"You were after *Sean*," she spat.

"Who, me?" Yes, I actually said, *Who me?* I was beginning to see Adam's point about me never winning an Oscar. "I was after Adam."

"You were after Sean. You watched him moonily all day Friday. You took an hour and a half for lunch, waiting for him to show up."

I raised my chin haughtily. "You people are slave drivers. Can't I have a break to watch *What Not to Wear?*"

"Besides," she said more calmly, examining me too closely for comfort, "if you and Adam really were about to start going out, Adam wouldn't have complained to me just yesterday about Sean stealing his girlfriend. He'd be happy to have you, and he'd forget all about her."

Good point. Where was Adam to take some of this heat? I looked around futilely for him. Then I told part of the truth. "It's the principle of the thing. Adam's also mad Sean broke his remote-control Hummer that he got for Christmas six years ago."

She went limp with exasperation. "*Adam* broke that! Adam said Sean broke it on purpose, Sean said Adam broke it, and I believed Sean."

"Exactly."

She stared me down, waiting for me to crack, while I tilted my head this way and that way and fluttered my eyelashes at her. Finally she nodded at the door and said, "You're in the warehouse. With Sean."

A torture worse than death, ho ho. A second chance to move things along. Sean and I helped the full-time workers take boats out of storage. Mostly we found the boats that needed to be brought down, cleaned the seats, and topped off the fluids in the engines. As we finished each boat, Cameron and my brother delivered it across the lake. Adam had gas. More than throwing me with Sean for spite, I think Mrs. Vader was trying to keep Sean and Adam away from each other.

I did my best with Sean, but it wasn't good enough. He treated me *exactly* like he always had, except for two days before in the boat. He would do things that were so, so sweet, like get me a soda from the office when he got one for himself. But then he spoke to an old lady customer in the same loving tone he'd used on me. Also his mother.

Maybe he didn't know yet that Adam and I were going out. I couldn't imagine Mrs. Vader had shared this tidbit with him if she thought it would add fuel to the fire. So Sean didn't understand he was supposed to realize I was girlfriend material and feel jealous. Skilled though I was in the womanly arts of manipulation and talking smack, I couldn't quite figure out a way to pass this info along to him without coming out and telling him, which would blow my cover. So I was super-sweet right back to him and traipsed around the warehouse in my tank top and generally acted like he and I were just friends. Ha!

Late in the afternoon we went wakeboarding. Yesterday we'd skipped calisthenics for the first time ever, and we had no taste for them today either. My brother didn't announce it was time for calisthenics, and neither did Cameron. Sean and Adam just glared at each other as they threw life vests at each other to pitch into the boat.

I think we all were a bit on edge by the time we launched. But Sean spotted first and Adam sat way up in the bow, so we began to relax. After all, Sean and Adam weren't likely to get into it on the boat. Cameron and my brother were there to pull them off each other. My brother was bigger than any of them.

As for me, I wanted so badly to sit across the aisle from Sean. He might scoot over and share my seat with me, like two days before. But no, he would never do this and mess up his "relationship" with Rachel—not while it was having the desired effect on Adam.

Subtlety and patience were not a couple of my strong points. Perhaps you have figured this out. However, I managed to keep my eyes on the prize, which meant bypassing the seat next to Sean and hunkering down against the wind in the bow with Adam. Problem was, Sean's seat faced backward so he could spot for my brother wakeboarding. He didn't even *see* the knee-weakening look Adam gave me as I sat down.

But Cameron in the driver's seat could see us, and Sean might be so gracious as to turn around once in a while. I wondered what Adam would want to do with me. Whether he would try to touch me, and where. Maybe he was thinking the same thing I was thinking: it was a bit early for PDA in our faux couplehood. If we suddenly fell in love after almost sixteen years of being friends, it would be *obvious* we were faking to show Sean we didn't care about him and the treacherous Rachel.

For whatever reason, Adam didn't touch me. He was content to watch me, darkly. I had no idea why he was looking at me this way. Clearly we were *not* thinking the same thing after all.

Then I had another problem. Adam had told me two days before that I'd screwed my chances with Sean by taking his place in the wakeboarding show. Maybe I should face-plant an air raley so Sean wouldn't think I was rubbing it in. But you know what? I was still so thrilled with my great runs two days in a row, I wasn't willing to throw it for a boy. Even a boy this important. Maybe this was something I could work on as I matured.

Sean had another bad run. Adam did too—ouch!—but at least he enjoyed it. I had another run so fantastic, I decided I'd work on an S-bend the next day. Ideally this would involve *landing* the S-bend, unlike some adrenalin junkies I knew.

And Sean didn't seem to mind I did well and he didn't. He was his usual pleasant self, a bit too distant for my taste, same-old, same-old. He must have *really* been basking in the fact that he'd gotten Adam's goat. I mean, girlfriend. That was okay. I would get Sean in the end.

I was feeling very hopeful about the whole situation when we docked at the marina. Maybe it was the sun again, or the lingering glow from my good run. But when Adam helped me out of the boat and we did the secret handshake, I didn't even care it was a complete waste of handshake because Sean had already gone into the warehouse and didn't see it happen. Doing the handshake made me feel like *somebody* valued me enough to do a secret handshake with me.

"By the way," I said during the high-five, "What was up with the look you kept giving me in the boat?"

"What look?" Adam asked, blushing. He knew what I meant.

"This look." I showed it to him.

He squinted at me. "I'm not a doctor, but I'd say either indigestion or a stroke."

We laughed, touched elbows, and parted

ways on the wharf. I sauntered to my house, taking big sniffs of the hot evening air scented with cut grass and flowers, not minding too much that I had to spend a few minutes blowing a gnat out of my nose. I wished Sean had asked me out like he was supposed to. But if I had to go on a fake date to get him, there was no one I'd rather go on a fake date with than Adam. I might even enjoy it, as friends.

After supper with Dad and McGillicuddy, and a luxe beauty routine that included teasing my mascara-coated eyelashes apart with the comb attachment to McGillicuddy's electric razor, I was ready. An hour early. I peered out my bedroom window at Adam's house and wondered what he was doing right now. Getting ready himself? Taking a shower?

Even though the picture of him in the shower was all in my head, I took a step back from the window at the force of the picture, and the realism. I must be picturing *Sean* in the shower, because the boy in the shower wasn't wearing a skull and crossbones.

Adam wore the skull and crossbones while wakeboarding and swimming. He must wear it in the shower too. Or did he?

In all the times over the years we'd worked together at the marina, when he'd bent down and the pendant had swung from the leather string, I'd never noticed a dirty patch in the shape of a skull and crossbones on his neck. Okay, I couldn't stand another hour of torturing myself this way.

I said *ta* to my dad and waded in my high heels down my yard to the dock. Then I untied the canoe and set off across the lake. Crossing the lake in a canoe, a sailboat, or anything without a motor could be harrowing. The lake was about a half mile wide at this point, and a canoe crossing the traffic pattern was likely to get T-boned by a speedboat driven by someone from Montgomery who didn't understand boating laws and was drunk to boot. But the busiest part of the day was over, and I paddled fast.

On the other side, I tied up to the Harbargers' dock. Funny that the kids weren't swimming. They'd probably been swimming all day and had brained each other several times with plastic shovels and nearly drowned once, and their nanny was about damned tired of it and had made them get out of the water. I was all too familiar with this scenario.

Sure enough, as I waded up their yard, I heard the kids laughing behind the fence. Even I, the Great Lori, Number One Seed Wakeboarder on the Vader's Marina Team, didn't think I could scale a wooden fence wearing high heels. Pitching one shoe over and then the other, I jumped up, grabbed the top of the fence, and hoisted myself up.

The kids were making castles in the sandbox. Really just mounds of sand, but I'm optimistic. Frances sat cross-legged in the grass nearby, wearing her summer hippie uniform: tie-dyed T-shirt, hemp shorts, bare feet. (Stuck in the grungewear of her college days in the early 90s, she also had a winter hippie uniform that involved wool and Birkenstocks.) She and the kids stared up at me.

I dropped down on their side of the fence, walked over, and sat on the edge of the sandbox. "Whatsamatter?" I asked the kidlets. "You've never seen such a vision of loveliness?"

"There's a gate, you know," Frances said.

"I didn't notice."

"It's on the other side of the house, off the driveway, where people usually put gates."

"I got in, didn't I? God, you always want

me to do things *your* way." This was sort of unfair. Frances had been pretty hands-off as governesses went. Like I had anyone to compare her to. "Well, this time I've definitely done something that isn't covered in the child care manual. Go ahead, ask me what happened at the party. Ask me what happened the night *after* the party. Ask me where I'm going now, dressed to kill."

The kids gaped at me when they heard the K word. Which probably didn't reassure them about their futures as well-adjusted teens under the instruction of Fanny the Nanny. It didn't help matters that while I told Frances about Sean and Adam, she placed her hands on her knees and began one of her deep-breathing relaxation techniques.

"Well?" I shouted. Her eyes flew open. I prompted her, "Doesn't this sound like a supreme girl-adventure? Do you watch *Laguna Beach*? That's a silly question, isn't it? Never mind. Maybe they have drama like this on *The NewsHour with Jim Lehrer*."

"Something else is going on with those boys," she said.

"Like what?"

"I'm not sure. It's been years since I gave Adam *or* Sean *or* Cameron *or* Bill the evil eye. You're the only one who comes to visit. Except . . . Mirabella, we do not eat the sand." She scooped up the girl and took her inside. The girl didn't protest. These children had been drugged or lobotomized.

I turned to the boy. "Don't you ever protest?"

He shook his head.

"Hold strikes? Write letters of complaint? She always told us we had permission to do anything if we could write a convincing argument for it. We tried."

He intoned in a cute little zombie voice, "We do not eat the sand."

Frances came back out and deposited the girl in the sandbox again. The girl examined some nearby dried leaves hungrily. "I guarantee you something else is going on there," Frances repeated. "Yours isn't the only plot."

"Right. Sean stole Rachel from Adam to get revenge. Sean is always the instigator of the plot. For the record, Sean is the one who started calling you Butt I Don't Need a Governess. I probably wouldn't have been half the hellion I was, if it hadn't been for Sean egging everybody on."

"I don't know," Frances said thoughtfully.

"It was Adam who set off the firecrackers in my homemade cheese."

"OH MY GOD I HAD COMPLETELY FORGOTTEN ABOUT THE HOMEMADE CHEESE." I laughed until I choked. The children studied me with serious eyes. They were adapting to the Montessori method a lot better than McGillicuddy and I had.

"I always loved Adam," Frances said.

I sniffled. "You *did*?" Frances wasn't too free with the professions of love.

"But Adam had room to grow. Sounds like he still does."

Feeling strangely defensive of Adam all of a sudden, I said, "*Everybody* has room to grow."

"And I don't want you to be his field." She gave me a stern look.

"What am I, a crop of rutabagas?"

She glanced at the kids and said through her teeth to me, "Do you understand?"

"Not really. Are you forbidding me to see Adam?" This was actually kind of romantic, though ridiculous. *I forbid you to see the boy next door!*

"Mirabella and Alvin," Frances said, "please turn on the garden hose and water your mother's beautiful flowers." Miraculously, the brainwashed kiddies stood and obeyed, taking half the sand with them. Frances watched them go, then turned to me.

"Ever since your mom died," she whispered, "your dad has been terrified for you kids. But he's gone out of his way not to be overprotective so that *you* don't live life afraid. And those were the instructions he gave me as your caregiver." She reached over and patted my knee. "No one's going to forbid you to do anything, Lori. Just . . . watch out around those boys."

Nine

Adam sat on the end of my dock with his shoes beside him and his bare feet swinging in the bryozoa-infested waters. Just kidding—my dock had been Sanitized for My Protection by a minnow net with a very long handle.

I skimmed the canoe against the dock and stopped myself with an oar. He stood up dripping, caught the rope I threw him, and wound it around the dock cleat. "Date or what?" he asked.

Grabbing my shoes from the bottom of the canoe, I confirmed, "Date. Ew. It's so weird to think about. Help me out, lovah."

He put out a hand to help me onto the dock. He did it in such a gentlemanly fashion, with no tickling or pinching or even a secret handshake, that I couldn't help but yank his arm to startle him. Then *he* put his weight on *me* to keep from falling, and we both came within a few millimeters of flipping the canoe over and landing in the lake.

We both managed to save at the last second. He helped me out of the canoe as if nothing had happened, except his face was bright red, and he wore that *don't make me laugh* look. "Your dad said you went to see Frances."

"Yeah. I told her about the plan, and she thinks you're only going along with it because you want to get lucky with me." We shared an uncomfy titter at this ridiculous idea as he slid his feet into his shoes, but something made me press him about this. "Did you get lucky with Rachel?"

He stared down at me, disapproving. He turned the disapproving stare in the general direction of the Harbargers' dock across the lake.

"You did," I said with a sigh. I hadn't realized I'd been holding my breath.

"N—," he started. "W— Mmph." He put both his hands into his hair. This showed me how strong and well-formed the biceps were on this tanned, beautiful boy. "I didn't, but you don't know that, okay? I have two older brothers. As far as they're concerned, I've been doing the entire cheerleading squad since I was fourteen."

He hadn't. So why was I picturing the tanned biceps straining as he braced himself above . . . who?

"Your dad's thinking the same thing," Adam said.

"About your biceps?" I chuckled.

Slowly and oh so painfully I realized no one had made a joke out loud about Adam's biceps.

Slowly and less painfully he put his arms down. "I would like some gum," he said. "Would you like some gum?"

"I would love some gum," I croaked.

He reached deep into the pocket of his shorts and drew out each of the following items in turn, placing them in his other pocket: his wallet, a lighter, a Sacagawea dollar, a plastic box of fishhooks, a four-inch-long pocketknife. Finally he produced a pack of gum so old, the company had switched to a new logo since it was made. Fine. Anything I could stuff into my mouth.

"I meant," he said, jaw working hard on a petrified square, "your dad thinks I want to get lucky with you too. At least, that was his second reaction when I rang the doorbell and told him I was there to pick you up for our date. His first reaction was to threaten to have me arrested."

"Oh, pshaw." I swallowed a mouthful of artificial flavoring. Mmmmm, igneous. "He threatens to have *me* arrested. It's a term of endearment." I walked down the dock so Adam would follow me. When I glanced back, he was still standing at the end of the dock. I threw over my shoulder, "I'll visit you in prison."

He jogged to catch up with me, and held my arm to balance me as I slipped my heels on. I knew better than to wear heels on the dock. I'd seen too many girls wear them at the boys' parties. Heels got caught between the planks and arrested forward motion, yo.

"Why didn't you tell your dad we're hooking up?" Adam asked. "I told my mom we're hooking up." He sounded almost hurt, like he thought I was embarrassed of him.

"Would you come off it? You shouldn't have told your mom. She gave me the third degree this morning, like she knows something's up between you and Sean. You tried to get her to *ground* him? How am I supposed to go out with him if she *grounds* him?"

Adam shrugged and said with a straight face, "If you really loved him, it wouldn't matter what you did when you went out, as long as you were together." He pressed his lips together.

"You are so full of it. Anyway, I told Dad you were giving me a lift to town to buy an eyelash comb tonight, and we might hang out for a while. I figured he'd stage an intervention if I told him the whole truth. And if I told him you and I were hooking up for real, he'd give me the *fourth* degree about it, and you, and *sex*, and . . . oh."

Adam nodded. "Whereas if you didn't tell him, he'd give *me* the *fifth* degree."

"I guess I didn't think it through. It didn't seem worth the trouble, since we'll only be together a couple of weeks." Truth was, I'd focused on how our diabolical plan would help me get Sean. With an emphasis on *Sean*. Not that Adam's relationship with my dad didn't matter, because they *did* have to live next door to each other for several more years, but come on. What were a few fake dates between friends?

We walked up the hill to Adam's driveway. I opened the passenger door of the pink truck and climbed inside—and I do mean *climbed*, because when I stood on the ground, the seat was even with my head. Adam sat in the driver's seat, weirdly. He'd driven McGillicuddy and me home from tennis the night before, but I was used to sitting in the backseat with Adam while someone older drove. I wasn't used to seeing him as a driver himself.

Sean's new truck had already left the driveway. He had to drive all the way across town to pick up Rachel. No worries. We'd see them at the movies. Our biggest problem would be deciding whether to sit on the back row with the other couples who planned to make out, or further down where Sean and Rachel could see us. Then maybe there would be the additional problem of the making out. But I was getting ahead of myself. We could solve that problem when we came to it, and we hadn't even reached the movie theater yet. We were taking a detour at the dirt track, probably to show some of Adam's friends the new (to him) pink truck. And the hot prize of a girl inside! Yeah, probably not.

Instead of parking in the dirt track lot, he drove around to the mud field. It was just a huge pit of mud that the owners of the dirt track lovingly sculpted into valleys and bumps, and watered daily. Build it and they would come. Boys loved to splash across the mud pit in their pickup trucks. They didn't do this with their girlfriends, though. Girls wouldn't put up with this.

And yet here we were, perched on the lip of the pit. Scooter Ledbetter pulled up behind us in his jacked-up F-150. We couldn't even back out.

I ventured to ask, "Is this our date?"

"In all its glory." With one arm, Adam made a sweeping motion across the mud field before us.

"Great. We're trying to make Sean and Rachel jealous, besides which it's my first date in real life, and you're taking me mud riding." I'd been with the boys and Mr. Vader to the dirt track countless times to watch races. I'd always thought my first date would be with Sean. Adam wasn't too far off. But I'd never imagined my first date would be with Sean's stand-in *at* the dirt track. "You're bringing sexy back."

He stuck out his bottom lip. "Where did you want to go?"

"Didn't Sean and Rachel go to the movies?"

"Yeah, but I'll bet she made him take her to the new Disney cartoon. That's his punishment for stealing her from me. That and *Laguna Beach*. Endless episodes of *Laguna Beach*." He cracked his knuckles.

"Adam, I don't care if it's *Mickey and Minnie Bust a Move*. We need to be there."

"We want to make them jealous," he agreed, "but we can't follow them around. We don't want to *admit* we're trying to make them jealous. And that's exactly what we'll be doing if we set foot in *Mickey and Minnie Bust a Move*."

I started to protest. But as I thought about it, I remembered every time I'd watched a DVD with the boys, Adam had left the room after thirty minutes, asking Cameron to call him back in for the juicy parts. And we were always telling Adam to be quiet. We couldn't hear the movie over his CD player, or his drum set, or the roar of the blender as he made milkshakes in the kitchen. I asked, "You can't sit through a whole movie, can you?"

He frowned, which made cute little lines appear between his brows. He fished the lighter out of his pocket and flicked it, studying the flame.

Either he couldn't sit through a whole movie, or it hurt him too much to be around Rachel while she was with Sean. This wouldn't help us make them jealous. But it *was* only the second night after the freaking shock of seeing Sean and Rachel together for the first time. Adam's heart must be breaking every time we talked about Sean and Rachel, yet he'd come with me this far. I could be more understanding and give him a few days for the wound to scab over.

"We don't have to go to the movie," I sighed, "but we need to go somewhere girls will see us. There's no one here but boys. It'll never get back to Sean and Rachel that we were together. Boys don't gossip."

"Pah! You don't know us as well as you think."

This was a disturbing prospect.

He stuffed his lighter back in his pocket. "Here's an idea. Call me crazy, but what if we actually *enjoyed* hooking up?"

"Whoa, Nelly," I said. "You scare me, thinking out of the box."

"What if we made hooking up *productive*?"

"That's what I'm talking about. Producing envy, with or without big fat teardrops."

"Forget about that, Lori. It'll come without us trying so hard." He took the box of fishhooks out of his pocket and rattled it. "You're turning sixteen in less than two weeks."

That was a low blow. "You don't have to rub it in that I forgot your birthday," I protested. "You remember mine because yours is first."

"And didn't your dad stop taking you for driving lessons after you ran his Beamer into the woodpile?"

"Only because he told me to back to the left, and I thought I did. I would have done fine if he'd pointed instead of telling me the direction. Again, you don't have to rub it—"

"I'll teach you to drive."

I blinked. He *was* a daredevil. "Around town?"

"No, right here. It's safer."

I pondered the mud field. "I might wreck the pink truck."

"Who could tell?"

"I might hit somebody else."

"If they're here, mud riding, they'd probably get off on it."

As if in agreement, Scooter Ledbetter chose this moment to start honking his horn in time to his stereo blasting Nine Inch Nails.

"Oh, what the hell," I said, spitting my petrified gum out the window. It had turned more of a metamorphic flavor anyway. I scooted into the driver's seat as Adam crawled over me. Nose close to his shirt, I caught a whiff of his cologne.

And then, too soon, he was on his side of the truck and I was on mine. "Is it in first gear?" he asked. "Are your feet on the brake and the clutch? Look both ways and make sure no traffic is coming before proceeding carefully into the mud hole."

I screamed like a girl as the edge of the pit fell away under us. Then I bit my scream off short as we bounced over a little hill and then a big hill that sent us flying. Now I was giggling.

Adam grinned and fastened his seatbelt.

"Put the truck in first gear again," he said in an amazing imitation of the calming announcer voice from the films we watched in driver's ed. "Press harder on the gas to scale the side of the mud hole. As you reach the top and circle back around for another turn, don't forget to signal."

Later, waiting in line for our seventh time through, he told me, "You drive fine."

"Really?" I squealed.

"Yeah. Of course, I haven't told you to turn left or right."

"Right," I said, disappointed. I thought I'd been driving fine, too. But I'd done well only because he hadn't asked me to do anything hard, like tell left from right. And let's not even *think* about starboard and port.

"When you're driving by yourself, it won't matter," he reasoned. "You've lived in this town forever. You know how to get around. Your dad won't be sitting in the passenger seat, telling you to turn left or right. The only time anyone will do that is when you take your driving test."

"That's also the only time a person taking her first road test will be banned from driving in Alabama for life." I edged the pink truck forward as a Dodge Ram dropped into the mud field in front of us.

"I have ADD," he said. "I'm the master of cheating on tests. Just put your hands on the wheel like this." He placed his hands on the dashboard with his first fingers up and his thumbs in, pointing toward each other. "*L* is for left."

"Won't the chick giving me the test notice I've got my fingers in an *L* on the steering wheel?"

"Hold your hands like that while she's examining your car," he said. "By the time you start driving, she won't think anything about it. She'll think you have arthritis and it's none of her business."

I looked over at him. "You're a lot sneakier than I thought."

He smiled.

I said, "Frances hasn't forgiven you for exploding her homemade cheese."

His laughter rang out at just the moment I plunged the truck into the pit. He'd given me the confidence of Dale Earnhardt Jr. on holiday. I veered off the very beaten path and into uncharted mud puddles. I kicked up splashes so high, Adam rolled up his window and asked me to roll up mine to save what was left of the ancient interior. We bounced from corner to corner and were bouncing our way back again when the truck dipped lower than I expected, sending a wave of muddy water across the hood and up the windshield. I pressed the gas and heard a ripping sound.

I turned to him in horror. "I broke your truck."

"We're just stuck. It happens." He unfastened his seatbelt. "Switch back."

I started to crawl over him. He'd crawled over me last time, and I figured this time he'd slide under. But he started to crawl over, too. We met in the middle, laughed, and both moved to slide under at the same time.

"Do you want to be on top or on bottom?" he asked.

"Either way," I heard myself saying. I had to remind myself that this was Adam, not Sean. This was the baby of the Vader family, who had always been the littlest, up until two days ago. At least in my mind.

He picked me up and, before I could wiggle, removed me to the passenger side. "There." He slid into the driver's seat and pressed the gas, harder than I'd pressed it, with a longer and louder ripping noise. He opened the door and stepped out, sinking much farther than he would have on solid ground. "They'll call a tractor from the racetrack to pull us out, but it might take a while. Let's wait by the concession stand. You'll ruin your shoes, though. Here, get on my back."

He stood outside the open driver's side door. His back was waiting. I hadn't been on a boy's back since . . . hmm . . . a free-for-all fight with girls on boys' backs at Cathy Kirk's pool party in middle school. If I'd been included, obviously there hadn't been enough girls to go around. And in middle school, the girls and boys were about equal in height and weight, so I'd worried I would crush the boy I rode on.

Not so with Adam. My shoes were dainty things you shoved your toes into with nothing to hold them on. I kicked them off and held them in one hand. I slid across the seat and onto his strong, solid back, feeling like a feather. A snowflake! A dainty snowflake surrounded by an acre of mud.

He nudged the door closed with his hip. I looked down. His feet had disappeared.

"What about *your* shoes?" I asked. "Your mom will kill you."

"They're Sean's. I'll put them in his closet just like this."

I felt a momentary pang for Sean. Then almost laughed out loud, picturing the look on his face. They were his shoes, and he would have a right to be mad. But if anything could ever make me dislike Sean, it was how much he cared about his clothes. I cared about my own clothes only through great effort.

Sean's shoes made a *schlep* sound every time Adam took a step. He struggled getting up the hill to the lip of the mud hole, and I thought I would have to dismount after all.

He felt me start to slide down. "No!" he said, catching my legs more tightly. "We're fine." With one last *schlep* we made it to the top. The prize was a tiny Airstream trailer blowing smoke out an exhaust fan. The air smelled like fried food. "Are you hungry?" he asked.

"No, but that never stopped me before."

"Me too." He stepped up to the window and looked in. "What'cha got?"

The clerk/cook/janitor looked up from a

NASCAR talk show on TV. "Cheese fries, homemade doughnuts."

With me on his back, Adam couldn't turn his head around enough to look at me, but he turned it enough to let me know I should choose from this array of delicacies.

"Strangely," I said, "I have a taste for cheese fries."

Adam reached into his pocket to pay. Putting me down on the bench beside the concession stand would have been miles easier. I was beginning to understand that he liked having me on his back. Holding my shoes in one hand, I grabbed the cheese fries with the other, and he carried a soda.

He walked to the bench, put the soda down, then put me down. I was still holding the cheese fries and my shoes. I tossed my shoes on the ground (oh well, so much for dazzling rhinestones) and picked up the soda so he could sit down, then handed it to him. It was like one of those problems on a standardized test at school. If Sean hooks up with everyone in school on Wednesday and Rachel on Friday, and Adam hooks up with Rachel on Thursday and Lori on Sunday, on what day does the nuclear war commence? One of those problems Adam would just draw an *X* through because he *thought* he would never encounter anything like it in the real world.

He crossed one leg over the other casually, as if he weren't coated with mud up to his knees. Then he took a sip of the soda, handed it to me, and pulled out a cheese fry. I took a tentative sip of soda. Not that I thought he had germs—or really bad germs, anyway—but we'd never shared a soda before. We'd shared popcorn, of course, while we watched DVDs with the other boys. Once the scoop from my ice cream cone had plopped into the lake, and he'd shared his ice cream with me. This was probably kind of gross. Mrs. Vader and Frances had rushed at us when they saw me about to take a lick. I shouldn't read too much into sharing a soda now, though. It was something people did when they went out.

"Mmph!" he hummed with his mouth full of cheese fry. Swallowing, he grabbed my bare foot and pulled it into his lap. "You painted your little toenails."

I opened my mouth to explain proudly that the toenails in question represented hours of meticulous work. Well, maybe forty-five minutes while watching reruns of

Deadliest Catch. I'd put the polish on and taken it off three times because it tended toward gloopy. Who knew beauty regimens would be so complex?

But when I looked up, my mouth just stayed open. He was staring at me with those light blue eyes. A chill hit me from nowhere. It made the hair on my arms stand up. It raced down my body to my toes, which he was stroking with one rough thumb. And so the chill moseyed back up my body again.

I took a slow, shaky breath through my wide open, ridiculously gaping mouth. Then I realized what the problem was. His resemblance to Sean was eerie sometimes, especially the light blue eyes. I managed to say, "You're giving me the look again. Don't look at me like that."

Stubbornly he gave me the look for ten more seconds, so there. I would be lying if I said I didn't enjoy the look. I *really* enjoyed what it did to my skin. He was a superhero with Massage-O-Vision. I enjoyed it too much for comfort. He was just going to turn his Massage-O-Vision on Rachel when he got her back, so the pleasant pricklies *I* felt were pricklies on loan. He'd be horrified to know he was giving them to me. Besides, I wasn't going to sit there and let him give me the look when I'd asked him not to give me the look.

Just as I was about to either pinch him or find the strength to look away, he let my toes go and turned away himself, gazing out over the splashing trucks. The mud sparkled in the artificial light. At first glance it might have seemed about as romantic as watching cement being poured, or a building being demolished by a wrecking ball. Nothing said *romance* like the scent of burning rubber. But to me, it started to seem very romantic. I almost wished Holly and Beige could see me now. Well, not really, because mud had splashed up on my calves. I scratched at a spot with my fingernail, and it smeared.

He asked, "Why does it have to be Sean?"

Ten

I snapped my head up and tried to gauge what he'd meant by this. I couldn't tell, because he wouldn't meet my gaze. Which was probably a good thing. I could feel myself flushing as my heart pounded.

I was attracted to Adam. Not as much as I was attracted to Sean, of course. That would never happen. But Adam had been so sweet and so fun, teaching me to drive. Tangling with me as we switched places in the truck didn't hurt either. Or carrying me on his back. I really enjoyed him carrying me on his back.

Did he mean, *Why does it have to be Sean instead of me?* And if he did . . .

Good God, what was the matter with

me? Adam didn't like me that way. He just hated Sean. He wanted to know why I was so stuck on *Sean*, of all people.

And I didn't like Adam that way, either. Not really. Flirting with him was fun, but that's all it was, and I was getting carried away. I needed to remember I was on a mission. I would tell him the whole truth about the mission. I owed him that much, since he'd agreed to help me by faking a relationship with me.

I munched a cheese fry and thought about Sean sashaying his way through the school lunchroom last spring, Beige on one arm, Holly on the other. Everyone turned to watch as he passed. People called out to him from the tables. All he needed was the paparazzi behind him. Also Beige or Holly needed a very small dog that got sick when it ate too much protein. I said simply, "Sean lights up the room."

Adam still wouldn't look at me. He tried to shake one fry loose from a cheesy clump. "I can see why you'd want to watch him, listen to him. Not why you'd want to *get together* with him. He lights up the room so bright that you would just be sitting there blinking, blinded." He gave up on freeing the fry and stuffed the whole cheesy clump in his mouth. Immediately he started picking through the pile for another, like he needed something to do with his hands.

"I've always wanted to be with him," I said. "Yeah, logically I can see the drawbacks, but I don't think you or anyone could argue me out of it. I need to find out for myself, because I've wanted this so long."

"Always," Adam muttered, tossing up a bit of fry and catching it in his mouth.

"Almost always. Actually, I can remember the very day it started." The mud field in front of us dissolved into a sun-splashed view of the lake through shady branches. The roar of monster trucks faded, replaced by birds chirping, and my mother's voice. "It was before Mom died. We were all really little. But I remember it so clearly. Your whole family was at my house for a cookout in the summer. I was with Mom and your mom up on the deck. I'd wanted to play with you boys, but Mom wouldn't let me.

"Your mom said I was such a lovely little girl, so ladylike and polite. That's what pricked my ears up, of course: the praise. But I kept playing like I wasn't listening in. Then your mom said I didn't always have to stay home. I was welcome to come over to your house to play whenever McGillicuddy came over. She called him Bill. Whatever. Now I was really paying attention, and holding my breath to see what Mom would say. All I'd dreamed about my whole little life was playing with y'all."

"Why?"

I snapped out of my daydream. I'd almost forgotten Adam was sitting there.

He put one hand on my knee, watching me, and didn't even turn to look when Scooter purposefully spun his tires, coating one side of the pink truck in mud. "Why did you want to play with us?" Adam asked. "At that age, we were basically squirting each other in the face with water guns."

"Compare this to sitting in my room by myself, dressing and undressing the Barbie."

"Oh." He nodded.

"Anyway, of course I was disappointed, as always. My mom said your mom was so nice to offer, but she didn't want me playing with four boys very often. I'd grow up to be a tomboy."

"What's wrong with growing up to be a tomboy?"

"I think it's fine until a certain age. When you're young, being a tomboy may even give you a certain advantage. You can always beat girls like Holly Chambliss and Beige Dupree and, ohmyGod, Rachel in Little League softball. You can catch four fish in the Girl Scout fishing rodeo while they're still refusing to bait their hooks because worms are icky."

"Rachel will actually bait her own hook," Adam defended her.

I didn't want to hear it. I talked right over him. "After a certain age, people don't know what to make of a tomboy, and you don't fit in. You end up feeling empty and lost."

Those frown lines appeared between his brows. He moved the plate of cheese fries behind him on the bench, slid over until his leg touched my leg, and put his hand on my knee again.

Strange how his touch made it easier for me to talk. I went on, "Just as Mom was telling your mom no, Sean came up the stairs crying. You and the other boys had dared him to stick bread between his toes and put his foot in the water. A fish mouthed him and he freaked out."

"Er—," Adam started.

I waved him off, because this was the most important detail. "My mom took his chin in her hand, turned his face toward me, and said, 'Just look at those eyes. He's going to be a heartbreaker.'" I found myself smiling at the memory. But when I turned to Adam and saw the look on his face, I stopped smiling.

"That sounds like a *bad* thing," he grumbled.

"People mean it as a good thing," I said, suddenly not as sure of this as I'd been for the last twelve years. But I couldn't really expect him to understand. Talking about Sean around Adam was like throwing Evian on a fire. "And then Mom said, 'Lori, just *wait* until you're sixteen.' She was stuck on the sixteenth birthday. We made a scrapbook with pictures of all my baby events, and spaces for when I would turn six and eight and ten and twelve, and a super-mondo sequined space for when I turned sixteen. She wanted me to have what she'd had, a great sixteenth birthday, exactly what any teenage girl would want. Her parents gave her a special grown-up ring, and she wore a groovy dress that's hanging in my closet."

We'd moved away from talking about Sean. Predictably, Adam took a deeper breath and relaxed against the bench. "Are you going to wear the dress on your birthday?"

"Are you kidding? It was the seventies. White polyester, baby. Highly flammable. Burn baby burn, disco inferno. Unsafe. Uncool."

"I'll bet it's pretty. You could wear it wakeboarding on your birthday, during the Crappy Festival show." He was back to his old self.

I chuckled. "Unfortunately, you and I are the only two people in the world who would think that was funny."

"What does that have to do with Sean?"

I squirmed a little under the gaze of the intense blue eyes. I felt his disapproval even though I hadn't told him what he should disapprove of yet. But he was helping me with Sean, and I'd committed to telling him the whole story. "Mom died not long after that. I took it as a free ticket to Disneyworld. Yay, Mom wasn't around to stop me! I got to play with the boys! Only I always felt guilty about being the least bit happy she was gone, even when this was the one good thing about it. And I felt guilty I didn't tell

Dad or Frances that Mom wouldn't have wanted me over at your house. It went against her wishes for me. I promised myself I'd clean up by the time I was sixteen. And if I could finally convince Sean to ask me out by my sixteenth birthday, I would know I'd turned out okay after all."

Adam nodded. "Because you think your mother picked Sean out for you."

"No, not exactly—"

"Like an arranged marriage," Adam interrupted. "That's very 2007."

"No, not like that. Mom knew what was best for me, and if she were still around, she would have taught me how to get it. She's not around, so I have to figure this out for myself. I'm transforming myself from an ugly duckling into a beautiful swan. There's much preening to be done. It's actually pretty time-consuming. I have to run my beak down every single feather to distribute the oil evenly and make myself waterproof."

"Lori—"

"And I've almost perfected my Holly/Beige imitation. At least, I *thought* I had, until the mud riding started."

"You think going out with Sean will turn you into Beige Dupree?"

"Sort of. If I hooked up with Sean, everyone would treat me differently. Everyone loves Sean. If Sean chose me, they'd think they'd always overlooked something special in me. Then maybe I really could become that girl. I know you hate Sean, but you understand why everyone else loves him, right?"

I took Adam's stony silence as a yes.

"Girlfriend/boyfriend love is totally different from brotherly love. But the effect would be the same. Like standing in his aura. Haven't you ever wondered what it would be like if Sean loved and valued you as a person?"

"I'd know Armageddon was coming. I'd brace myself for the locusts."

"I'm serious. If he just looked at you the right way, that alone could probably carry you through for a month. But if he *loved* you . . ."

Adam shifted on the bench. I thought he was standing up to stalk away, disgusted. Instead, he placed his arm around my shoulders. Lightly his finger stroked valentines on my arm, which gave me the shivers all over again.

"Every word out of Sean's mouth is

meant to hurt me," he said. "And it's always been like that. Cameron says Sean changed after I was born. When I was a baby and Mom wasn't looking, Sean threw blocks at my crib."

I almost laughed. The idea was so ridiculous. It was even more ridiculous for Adam to be angry about something like that when he was sixteen years old.

I managed not to laugh. I believed him. I knew Sean.

"But that's you," I said. "I'm sorry he treats *you* that way, but I'm the one who's going to get together with him, and he doesn't treat *me* that way."

"He will," Adam said. "If you ever let him get close to you, he will." The valentines he traced on my arm had turned to shapes with lots of sharp points, like in comic books when the superhero punches the villain. Ker-POW!

The tractor arrived then to pull the pink truck out of the mud. Adam took his hands off me—which I regretted more than I should have. He leaned forward to watch and make sure the driver didn't attach the chain to the loose side of the front bumper.

"Why does it have to be Rachel?" I asked.

"It just does," he said without taking his eyes off the truck.

"You might feel better if you talked about it."

"I doubt it."

"What do you like so much about her?"

When he turned to me, he seemed alarmed, as he had at the tennis court the night before. With wide eyes, he searched my eyes for something—which I probably would have given him, if I'd known what he was looking for. I asked, "What are you looking for?"

He shook his head and turned back to the mud pit. "I like her because she's so pretty," he said in his bullshit voice.

"That's no fair. I gave you a straight answer about Sean."

The tractor started forward. The chain to the pink truck pulled tighter and tighter and broke. One end of it flew over the tractor, barely missing the driver.

"She's cute," Adam said. "She has a nice ass. I don't know."

Now I understood. Talking about her hurt him too much. It was easier for him to pretend the ADD had kicked in.

After two more chains and a rope, the

tractor liberated the pink truck, and Adam bought the driver a doughnut. Adam and I drove through the mud field for another hour and a half, taking turns. Mostly we managed to forget Sean and Rachel.

Then we drove into town and hit all the teenage haunts: the arcade parking lot, the bowling alley parking lot, of course the movie theater parking lot. In theory this is exactly what I wanted. I was being seen out with Adam, in Adam's truck. In practice, Adam had purposefully besmirched Sean's pink truck with mud. It was like he wanted to be seen around town in it for that reason.

We rolled home at two minutes before my curfew. I'd figured he'd park the truck at his house, and I'd walk home. I was thrilled that he drove over to my driveway to drop me off. Sean wasn't home yet to see us, but maybe someone in the Vaders' house would watch across the yard and mention it to Sean later.

And then, as I was turning to Adam to thank him for teaching me to drive and allowing me to foam at the mouth about my mom, he bailed out the driver's side door. He walked around the front of the truck. I think he would have opened my door, a gentleman on a date, if I hadn't opened it first. It was too strange. I jumped to the ground, forgetting I was wearing my heels again. He caught me just before I pitched over onto the gravel.

"I'll—walk—you—to—the—door," he said slowly and clearly, like talking to someone who didn't speak English. Or didn't go out with boys much, or, like, ever. He took my hand. We walked toward the lights slanting through the shadows of pine trunks. Tree frogs screamed in the night, and the air was wet. I shivered.

We climbed the steps to the porch. Dad hadn't turned on the overhead light there, thank God. Adam stood close to me in the darkness, over me, expecting something. I expected something, too. I couldn't have stood the disappointment if we'd done all we'd done that day, hugging and giving each other smoldering looks and all, without something to show for it at the end, even if we *were* just friends. But my head felt too heavy to raise my chin.

"Hey." He put his hand under my chin and gently raised it for me. "If one of us were in love with the other, if it were uneven in some way, that would be bad." He gave me a long look I couldn't really see. The shadows on the porch were too deep. His eyes only glittered a little in the starlight.

I tried to give the look right back to him. "But we're not," I said, and what was that damned high squeakiness in my voice on *not*? I cleared my throat.

"But we're not," he agreed. "We have nothing to worry about. We can do whatever we feel like."

"Right," I said, and meant it.

The kiss was simple. He bent down and pressed his lips to mine. We stood still except for his pressure on my lips. But inside, every cell in my body turned a back flip to blind.

"Good night, Lori," he whispered. He bounced back to the pink truck, cranked the engine, drove one hundred feet to his own driveway, waved to me, and went inside his house.

I stood on my porch and stared at his house for a long time, telling myself that I did not like Adam that way because I liked Sean and Adam liked Rachel and *I did not like Adam*. It was just that Adam was very smart, and was second only to Sean at making confusing things sound simple and death-defying stunts seem like a good idea.

Eleven

Monday night, Dad insisted that Adam come over for dinner. Adam, my dad, my brother and I ate and joked together like we normally would out in the yard, except that it wasn't normal. It was weird. Adam sat in my mom's chair at the table. We might as well have been staring at a showy centerpiece made of silk flowers and hand grenades.

Tuesday night was much more comfy. Sean was over at Rachel's and Cameron was out with his girlfriend, so Adam and I had the Vaders' living room to ourselves to watch a DVD. At least, that's what we did for about thirty minutes. Then we played CDs in his room, experimented with his drum set, and made milkshakes in the kitchen. Without anyone else around to show off for, we could just be ourselves. Friends.

Wednesday night we went mud riding. I wore my sensible shoes this time—rubber flip-flops that could be hosed off. I knew this wouldn't sound very romantic when it got back to Sean or Holly or Beige. I also knew that, just like the other nights, I would stand on my porch with Adam and get the simplest, most shiver-inducing kiss. And then it would be over. The next morning, we'd go back to being friends.

Thursday night we scored. So to speak. We'd planned to go to the arcade and see who could kick the other's ass on the snowmobile racing game, but Adam called me just before it was time to pick me up. He sounded tinny, like his hand was cupped over his mouth and the receiver. "Code green. Code green. Rachel and Sean watching DVD here tonight. Over."

The wound Rachel had inflicted on him must have healed enough that he could stand being around her and Sean. Or he must miss her so much that he was willing to take a more active role in making her jealous. Either way, this was our big chance!

Slamming down the phone, I rushed upstairs to exchange my Skechers for Steve Madden pumps and my tank top for something that said elegance, sophistication, Express. This was how I was supposed to talk about clothes, right? Naming the brands as if I cared? Another coat of mascara and a run-through with the comb attachment to McGillicuddy's razor and I was ready, baby. Snap!

Sean's truck was parked in the driveway behind the pink truck. He'd already brought Rachel over. I swallowed and tried to slow down my breathing as I pressed the doorbell with one shaking finger.

Almost immediately, I heard Adam bouncing inside. He jerked the heavy door open. "What are you doing? You don't have to ring the doorbell, dork."

Dumbass! He'd called me a dork loudly enough for the Thompsons to hear three houses over. Talk about romance.

I was about to whisper acidly that he wasn't doing a very good job of falling head over heels in love. Then I noticed he was wearing his black T-shirt printed in white with a life-size rib cage. Adam looked best in black. The color reflected darkly in the hollows under his high cheekbones, not to mention the bruise under his eye, and made his strange light eyes stand out that much more. The skull and crossbones glimmered at his neck.

He raised his eyebrows, waiting for me to say what I'd opened my mouth to say.

I was speechless. So I grabbed his arm and spun him around at the same time. He was surprised. I managed to pin his arm behind his back for about two seconds before he shook loose and grabbed me.

"Now you've asked for it." He scooped me up, threw me over his shoulder, and held both my wrists in one hand so I couldn't tickle him. He kicked the door closed and hiked into the living room.

Pausing, he took a few steps toward Sean and Rachel watching TV on the sofa. They sat close together in the dark room. I wouldn't have been able to tell whose limbs were whose, except Sean didn't shave his legs. There was a loveseat where Adam and I could have settled. Then Adam thought better of it—too close for comfort—and hiked across the room.

"Hello, Sean. Good evening, Rachel," I called cordially, upside down.

Rachel gave us a half-hearted pipsqueak greeting. Sean shouted at us, "Can you keep it down?"

Hmph! Clearly he was in a jealous rage. Adam and I exchanged a knowing look as he slid me onto the desk in the corner. Still holding my wrists immobile, he fished in a drawer and brought out a long object.

I squinted at it in the dark. "Not the stapler!" I cried.

He grinned, tossed the stapler beside me, and rummaged in the drawer again.

"Please," I gasped, "not the Liquid Paper!"

"Shut up!" Sean shouted.

Adam and I widened our eyes at each other like we were offended and hurt. I shook my wrists out of his grasp and reached behind me for a red Sharpie out of the pencil cup. Smoothing my hand across his chest (shiver), I made a red mark across the bottom right rib printed on his T-shirt, the rib I knew he'd broken. Or was it my other right? "What ribs have you broken?"

He looked down at his shirt. "This one," he said, pointing.

I made a red mark across that rib. "What else?"

"Mm." He stretched his shirt out at the bottom so he could see it better, and pointed to the opposite side. "These two." He watched as I made neat red marks across those ribs. His chin was close to my cheek.

"Both of you act crazy," Sean said smoothly, "like you're off your medication. Or like you're going to a shrink."

I didn't look at Adam. I didn't think I looked at Sean, either. But I had an impression later of Sean's face glowing white and then blue in the light of TV, and Rachel in the shadows beside him. I thought the medication comment was meant for Adam. I knew the shrink comment was meant for me.

I capped the marker and stuck it back in the pencil cup. "I'll see you later," I whispered, sliding around Adam and hopping down from the desk. I had to get across the room and outside without being further humiliated, which meant I *must not* fall down in my high heels. Or cry. I even closed the front door behind me without making any noise.

And then Adam burst through it and

slammed it behind him, shaking the house. "Lori!"

"Shhh," I said with my finger to my lips, backing off the porch and into the wet grass. I didn't want to shout about what Sean had said. It was bad enough when we were quiet about it.

Adam collected himself as I watched, taking a deep breath through his nose, with his eyes closed. Then he opened his eyes and said, "The five-minute date does nothing to make them jealous." He formed his first finger and thumb into a circle. "Zero."

I swallowed. "I can't."

He stepped closer to me. "Sean has a way of finding that one thing that will make you feel so good about yourself, or so bad about yourself. That's why you love him. That's why I hate him. You knew this when you went fishing."

I was too discombobulated to make a joke about my lures. I just wanted to get away from their house. "I've had enough of boys for today, I think."

He frowned. "Are you sure?" He rubbed my arm. My hair stood on end.

Shivering in the warm night, I put my arm down by my side, where he couldn't reach it. "Too much of a good thing. It's strange, but even cheese fries can get tiresome."

"I'll walk you home, then."

"No," I said, "I'm sorry. I'm just done."

He watched me carefully for a moment, lowering his head to look into my eyes. "Okay. I'll see you tomorrow."

"Bye."

He walked back into the house and closed the door softly.

I stared at the door knocker, tree frogs screaming all around me. I had done the wrong thing. I wanted to be in the house with him. And Sean.

Sean had said something like that to me only once before, just a good-natured joke as we passed each other in the hall at school. I'd started to cry. The office had called my dad (again). Dad and McGillicuddy and I had had a Big Talk about it that night, wherein I told my dad that my business was not his to tell Sean's parents about, and wherein McGillicuddy promised to have a discussion with Sean about keeping his mouth shut. Apparently he had, because Sean never said a word to me about it again. And if he told the whole school, they were very discreet and didn't let on to me that they knew. Which would have been out of character for them, because they were bitches.

That first time happened not long after I went to the shrink, so Sean probably was just experimenting to see what I'd do. This time, he must have mentioned it because he was trying to hurt me. And if he'd tried to hurt me, he was in love with me and jealous of Adam. I knew this because when he *wasn't* in love with me and jealous of Adam, he ignored me and was quite pleasant to me.

Therefore, the plan must be working! Hooray! So I should go back in there, flirt with Adam, and press the issue.

As I stood there, considering whether to ring the doorbell or just walk on inside like I owned the place, or like they'd installed a dog door, I heard Adam holler, "Thanks, Sean."

"No problem," Sean said more quietly, because he was too courteous to yell in Rachel's ear.

I felt a flash of panic. They weren't being sarcastic. Adam was genuinely thanking Sean for getting him out of spending an evening with me. This was called a *negative self-concept*. I had learned about it in health class (tenth grade). Having a negative self-concept made me think people were making fun of me, on top of the times when they really *were* making fun of me, which I seemed to miss completely.

Then footsteps pounded up the stairs inside. Adam's bedroom light flicked on. He put his hands on the windowsill and pressed his forehead to the glass, looking for me, but he couldn't see out because of the glare.

Adam wouldn't double-cross me.

Would he?

Friday I had gas. This was fine with me. I spent most of the morning by myself on the dock, soaking up rays and feeling mentally diseased.

I didn't think I could stand a lunch hour in the office, eating Mrs. Vader's chicken salad sandwich, on edge, expecting Sean to sneak in or Adam to burst in or both. I told Mrs. Vader I was treating myself to a nice lunch out.

"Oh," she said, nodding. "Something happened between 'you and Adam'?" She moved her fingers in quotation marks.

Yeah, I didn't have the energy to argue

with her this time. That was Adam's problem. I walked over to my family's dock and launched the canoe.

The open water was choppy with wind and wakes from passing speedboats. I didn't get T-boned. It was a little early for anyone to be drunk.

The wind blew me off course. I reached the far bank and needed to backtrack along the shore to the Harbargers' house. Here in the shallows, protected by overhanging trees, the water was clear and calm. Miniature whirlpools stirred around my oar. I dragged my hand in the warm water, and minnows nibbled my fingers.

I docked at the Harbargers' and ran up to the house. It was such a relief to feel the grass on my bare feet! Every toe had a blister from a different pair of high-heeled sandals. I slid open the glass door and stepped into the den.

Frances and the kids looked up. They were sitting on the floor around the coffee table. Frances didn't sit on furniture if there was a floor available. A copy of *Mother Earth News* lay open in front of her. She had stuck lengths of uncooked spaghetti into balls of Play-Doh. The kidlets were busy sliding

Froot Loops onto the spaghetti, sorting by color. I couldn't believe they'd fallen for that old trick. Frances could convince children anything was a game, for about five minutes. Obviously some children were more gullible than others.

I walked into the kitchen and looked in the refrigerator. No surprises there. The meat loaf was made with tofu. Frances's strong points as a nanny included a master's degree in early childhood education and a PhD in Russian literature, but nothing approaching cooking skills, unless it was some weird hippie experiment like drying fruit on the roof. Mmmmm, rubbery apricots with a hint of tar. I filled a bowl with Froot Loops, poured soy milk over them, and joined the powwow on the floor.

Between bites I asked, "What did you mean when you said mine wasn't the only plot?"

Without looking up from the magazine on the coffee table, Frances said, "I told you. I don't know."

"What would be the metaphorical firecracker in the metaphorical homemade cheese?"

She shrugged.

"Like, Sean dared Adam to hook up with me because I'm so oafish and dog-looking?"

"You are *not* dog-looking," Frances said sternly. "Besides, a plot like that would involve a high level of organization. They would have to think it through carefully. None of you do that. Except Bill, of course, who thinks things through so carefully that he can't take action. Like his father."

My spoon stopped in my mouth at the mention of my dad, who'd been the farthest person from my mind. I swallowed and shouted, "Then what the hell kind of plot are you talking about?"

Frances didn't even react when I cussed in front of her charges. She reasoned that making a big deal out of curse words drew attention to them and caused children to use them more. So she ignored them. I'm not sure this ploy worked, but then, she'd had an uphill battle with McGillicuddy and me. We lived next door to Mr. Vader, who could have written a dictionary of filth. She asked, calm as ever, "Have you thought Adam might really like you?"

The hair on my arms stood up, just as if Adam were sitting behind me with his hand on my shoulder.

"No, I haven't." That would be seven kinds of awful, if Adam had agreed to pretend to get together with me because he *really* wanted to get together with me. My ploy to get Sean would be ruined. I might finally land Sean, like in my dreams. But knowing I'd broken Adam's heart would be a downer and a distraction. Like making out in the movie theater, knowing the pink truck in the parking lot was on fire. My mother wanted me to be with Sean, but didn't she want me to be happy?

Frances turned the page. "Open your eyes. And watch out for those boys."

Twelve

Wakeboarding that afternoon, I watched the boys until my eyeballs hurt from the sun glinting off the water. I could have sworn there was nothing to watch out for. Sean was a little warmer to me than usual—the way he always acted after he'd insulted me, like some friendliness here could make up for a lack of friendliness elsewhere.

Adam was *very* warm to me. While Sean drove, my brother wakeboarded, and Cameron spotted, Adam pulled me into his lap in the bow. He set his chin on my shoulder and rubbed his hands up and down my thighs. The best part of this, for the purpose of making Sean's blood boil, was that Adam did it without comment, without expecting me to comment, as if it were the most natural thing in the world for him to act like my boyfriend.

The worst part of this, for the purpose of watching out for those boys, was that if my eyelids had been duct-taped open to my eyebrows, I *still* wouldn't have been able to tell whether Adam liked me, or pretended to like me, or liked me but pretended he was only pretending.

The five of us pitched the wakeboards and life vests from the boat back into the warehouse. The Friday night party would start soon, so Sean, Cameron and my brother headed for the houses. I ought to have been right behind them. I needed plenty of time to shower and primp and change clothes twenty times like girls were supposed to do before parties.

But I took Adam's hand and held him back from the others. I whispered what had been bugging me all day. "Frances thinks you have a plot, other than the plot with me to make Sean and Rachel jealous."

His eyes flew wide open, and the rest of him seemed to shrink back a bit. Then he stood up straighter, and his brow went down. "Frances? I haven't spoken to Frances in years. Plus she's creepy."

"Only because she's always right," I said. "And last night, something you said to Sean . . . Do you have a plot against me? Are you double-crossing me? He dared you to go out with the dog next door, and if you did, he'd give you your cute little girlfriend back?"

He snorted, then seemed to have a hard time huffing out laughter, almost as if he were *relieved.* He snatched me to his tanned chest, hugged me hard, and breathed into my wet hair, "You're not a dog. You're beautiful."

Right. I knew what he meant. Beautiful on the inside. I *had* saved a baby sparrow or two in my time. I was not someone he would want to *hook up* with, but a beautiful person. Hooray.

"Don't ever let Sean convince you you're not." He glanced in the direction Sean had gone. "Let's go for a sailboat ride."

I loved sailing. But if we went now, we'd be late for the party. "Can't we do it tomorrow?"

"This will be an investment in your future. It'll be worth it."

I waited while Adam leaned into the

office to tell Mr. Vader what we were doing, and I followed him back into the warehouse. The sailboat was very old and very small. The hull was a light fiberglass platform with a hole for the metal mast. Adam and I toted the hull, mast, and sail to the edge of the wharf, threw them in, and tossed down a couple of life vests. Adam stepped carefully onto the hull, sat down, and steadied it against the concrete wall for me as I stepped on and sat down. The sitting down was very important. The boat was so small that it would tip and throw us off if we shifted our weight the slightest bit too far, like trying to stand on a basketball. Together we lifted the mast upright, slid it into the hole in the center of the hull, and unfurled the red sail.

"Do you want to drive?" he asked.

"You can drive," I said.

I scooted around the mast to the tiny bow. Adam slid to the back, taking the rope attached to the sail in one hand and the handle of the rudder in the other. He pulled the sail taut, the wind filled it—and the boat tipped over, dumping us both into the lake.

I came up quickly. The life vests were floating away on the current, but the more important thing was to make sure the mast didn't fall out of the hole and sink. We'd have a hard time retrieving it from the bottom of the lake, even here near the wharf where it was relatively shallow.

Adam had the same idea. Without a word to each other, we met under the boat. His hair floated weirdly around him and his blue eyes were bright in the dark green water as he motioned for me to turn the hull right side up while he dove after the slowly sinking mast.

I came up into the sunshine for a breath and flipped the hull. Adam surfaced beside me, groaning with the weight of tugging the sail full of water. Together we managed to bundle it around the mast so less water was trapped in it. We pulled the sail and mast out of the water, slipped the mast into the hole in the hull, and peeled the sail into position. Water rained everywhere.

"This is romantic," I said. "You have a knack. What the hell kind of date *is* this?"

He laughed. "You'll see."

After we retrieved the life vests, I sat on the bow like in *Titanic*. But without any of that *I'm queen of the world* bullshit, holding my arms out. Come on, it was a sailboat on a lake. Adam steered us back and forth across the water. The red sail billowed above us in the strong breeze, so we wouldn't get T-boned by drunks. Unless of course they headed straight for us like in a bullfight.

Sometimes Adam jerked the boat around so fast that I slipped off the bow and into the water. Dunk! These were not accidents, I thought—the gleam in his blue eyes was too gleamy. He turned the boat only when we were very close to shore, though, where it was safe. I wasn't too concerned about getting ground to bits by a passing boat motor in the open water.

We made it to the bridge and floated under. The sound of cars zooming on the highway overhead echoed in a sucking sound underneath, with a *clack-clack, clack-clack* as they crossed from one section of bridge to another. I called over the noise, "How much farther are we going?" I looked back at the Vaders' house, tiny across the water. "The party will start soon."

"Someone there you want to see?"

I thought he sounded bitter. But when I turned around to glance at him, he was the usual Adam, quiet and intense, one finger tapping the boat with barely contained energy.

"Yes, duh. Isn't there someone at the party *you* want to see? We can't make them jealous if we're not there."

"Actually, we can." He nodded to a pile. "Catch that and stop us."

I hugged the pile and brought the sailboat alongside it. Adam opened the compartment in the hull and pulled a can of spray paint out of the pool of water inside. He popped off the cap, sprayed a little paint into the air as a test, and stuffed the can into the waistband of his board shorts. "Wait here, woman," he said, then grinned. He climbed the pile, finding tenuous footholds between the concrete blocks.

"Uh," I said. He was already at the top of the pile. "Adam?" He reached to the metal outside edge of the bridge (thank God this side faced away from the setting sun, or it would have been too hot to hold) and, using only the strength of his arms (thank God for calisthenics), hoisted himself up until he stood on the ledge. All I could see of him was his heels peeking over the edge.

I wasn't worried about him falling. Cameron had fallen off before, and it had only stung. I *was* worried about the black clouds creeping up on the sun on the far side of the bridge, and the wind picking up. A cold gust caught the sail. The boom swung around suddenly and would have decapitated me if I hadn't ducked. Not really, but I would have had a blue bruise across my neck, and how sexy is *that*? I crawled to Adam's spot in the back of the boat, untied the rope, and lowered the sail. "Hey, Adam."

The clouds blotted out the sun. Far across the lake, the shoreline looked misty with a wall of rain. Lightning forked from the black clouds to the dark green lake.

"Adam, lightning!" I called. My voice was drowned by thunder.

The paint can dropped into the lake. I fished it out and put it back in the compartment. Lightning flashed, closer.

His feet appeared, his legs, his board shorts. With the strength of a hundred push-ups a day, he lowered himself slowly until he hung by his arms from the edge of the bridge. I expected him to drop into the water, because he was like that. He would be electrocuted, just to paint our names on the bridge. Which might sound romantic, except something could sound only so romantic when it involved spray paint.

Thankfully, he swung his legs onto the pile and descended the way he'd gone. He stepped carefully onto the boat just as lightning cracked again, so loud and bright we both jumped, and thunder boomed directly overhead. I scooted toward the bow to make room for him.

He raised the sail, saying, "I'm sorry."

"It's okay!" I shouted over the noise of the rain and the deafening echo of rain under the bridge. "Not your fault."

"It wasn't supposed to rain tonight."

"Storms pop up in the summer."

Pushing the sail into the wind just long enough to give the boat momentum, and pointing the sail out of the wind again before we blew over, he steered us toward shore. Two piles spanning the width of the bridge stood between us and the bank. Twice, we both put our hands on the piles to pull the boat out into the rain and around to the other side. I bent my head under the cold deluge. Big, hard raindrops beat the back of my neck.

We made it to shore and climbed part way up the slanted concrete embankment under the bridge. Adam brought one of the ropes from the boat with him. He curled it around his ankle so the howling wind didn't blow the boat home without us. I curled it around my ankle, too, for good measure.

We both stared forward at the swaying sailboat, red sail puddled on the hull, and the pile beyond it. Rain cascaded off both sides of the massive bridge in sheets. My bikini bottoms didn't provide much padding between the rough concrete and my ass. The rain had chilled me. I moved imperceptibly (I hoped) toward Adam to bask in his heat.

The noise and echo of the rain filled my ears, but Adam's voice beside me sounded even louder. "Why'd you go to the shrink?"

I looked down. My palm was bleeding. I must have scraped it on the pile.

"Was it because of your mom?"

I wiped my palm on my other hand. Great, now I had blood on both hands. Helpful. I wiped them on the back of my bikini bottoms. Blood stains came out in cold water, and we had plenty of that.

I could feel Adam watching me.

"It wasn't right after my mom died," I said. "Actually it wasn't until sixth grade, when Frances left because McGillicuddy and I had gotten too old to need keeping during the day while Dad was at work. Frankly, I think she was glad to go. Sean calling her Butt I Don't Need a Governess probably got tiresome."

"Sean gets tiresome in general." Adam didn't meant to change the subject—he just couldn't help making this comment. He tapped my knee with his knee, prodding me to go on.

"It wasn't like I did anything so crazy," I said. "Though that's probably what crazy people always say, right? I just didn't want to sit in class anymore. The teachers were fine and the kids were fine. I just couldn't picture myself sitting in a desk in a straight line of desks for another seven hours."

"Ha!" Adam said. "You had ADD."

"It must have been catching. So when Dad dropped me off at school in the morning, I started checking in at homeroom, then disappearing into the basement, or into the attic. I could stand over the ductwork at one corner of the attic and hear everything the principal said in her office. I could crawl above the auditorium, where the janitor went to change the spotlight bulbs, and listen to rehearsals of the school play. I was seeing this whole side of the school that other people didn't know existed."

Lightning flashed, thunder clapped. The rain pouring off the bridge into the lake sounded like static. That's what sitting in class back then had been like. Where there had been a channel before, now there was only static. I couldn't tune in, and even if I could, there was nothing to see.

"Eventually the school called my dad to say I'd missed so much school, I was going to flunk the sixth grade. My dad threatened a lawsuit because it was the school's fault they'd lost me. The upshot of it was that I went to a shrink for a while, and took some pills—"

"Pills," Adam said in utter disgust, like I would say *bryozoa* or *gelatin salad.* I hated gelatin salad. It was so ambiguous. What was it made of?

"These pills weren't bad," I said. "They helped. I only took them for a while. I went back to class and everything was fine. Really I think it never would have happened if you'd been in my class, if I'd had someone to talk to. The other kids didn't even notice I was gone."

We listened to the rain for a few moments. He said, "Lately I've been thinking about going back on my pills."

I thought he was saying this to make me feel better about spilling my secret. I *hoped* he was just saying this. Adam on his pills was no fun. He was serious and level-headed and cautious. Like everybody else. But if that's what he wanted, I should support him.

"Sean makes me . . . ," Adam said slowly, balling his hands into fists, ". . . so . . . mad." He flexed both hands with his fingers splayed. Like the anger was so great, he needed to shoot it out his fingertips before it caused him to burst into flames.

"I know," I said. "Me too." This wasn't exactly true. Sean didn't make me mad at him. He made me mad at myself.

A cool blast of wind made the chill bumps stand up higher on my arms. The sailboat rope tugged at my foot. I crossed my arms in front of me, covered as much skin as possible with my hands, and contracted into a ball.

"Hey. Come here." Adam slid his bare arm around my bare shoulders. Assuming we were both 98.6, I didn't understand how he could be so much warmer than me. His skin felt like he'd been standing in front of a fire. I slid my arm around his waist, too, and relaxed into his toasty goodness. I leaned my head against his shoulder. His fingers moved a little on my arm. I thought I heard his heartbeat speed up, but I wasn't sure.

Eventually the rain dwindled like someone turned down the volume of the static on TV. The thunder moved far away, and what was left of the sunset flung pink and orange on the scattering clouds. I hardly shivered as we edged down the embankment to the boat. Now the problem was finding any wind at all to get us home in the calm after the storm. Sitting on the hull, we both ducked as he wound the boom all the way around the mast and finally caught a little breeze.

We emerged from darkness under the bridge, into the golden light, and looked back. Partly because rain had battered the wet paint, and partly due to Adam's atrocious handwriting, the bridge didn't say ADAM LOVES LORI. I cocked my head to one side, then blurred my eyes, neither of which helped. I read out loud, "AOAN LOVES LOKI."

"They'll know what I meant." He was so proud. "Let Sean top that."

And he did.

Thirteen

The party had started. It was hard to see in the twilight, and with the mist rising off the water around us after the rain. But the gray twilight and gray mist made colors pop. Bright T-shirts and Slinky Cleavage-Revealing Tops dotted the Vaders' lawn and concentrated at the end of the dock. The faint bass beat of the music across the water was punctuated by the occasional *foop* of a bottle rocket.

Just as Adam had been waiting for me on my dock last Sunday when I canoed to see Frances, Mr. Vader was waiting for us on the marina dock. It was awkward generally for someone to wait for you on the dock like this, because you realized they were waiting for you and watching you when you were still ten minutes from reaching them. With Adam, I'd felt compelled to wave and make faces at him the whole return trip. With Mr. Vader, it was worse. He stood on the dock with his feet planted and his arms folded.

"I'm in trouble," Adam said.

"I know." I was sitting across from Adam on the hull. I didn't sit on the bow, and I didn't want to. It seemed inappropriate and frivolous now that Adam was about to get grounded.

We sailed past Mr. Vader on the dock. He followed us up the stairs and around the wharf. He helped us pull the mast and sail and then the hull out of the water and carry them, dripping, into the warehouse, all in complete silence. Mr. Vader's jaw was set. In the twilight, Adam's expression had already settled into darkness.

Finally Mr. Vader closed the door of the warehouse, locked it, and turned to face Adam with his hands on his hips.

"It wasn't supposed to rain tonight," Adam said quickly.

Mr. Vader nodded. "The storm popped up."

Adam backed off a millimeter. "Well.

Since you were paying attention, thanks for coming to our rescue."

"I knew you were okay. I watched you." Mr. Vader took a pair of folding binoculars out of his pocket.

"That's creepy," Adam said.

"You know what's creepy?" Mr. Vader asked. "Two kids who are supposedly dating spray-paint their names on the bridge like they're in love. They get caught under a bridge during an electrical storm. And they don't fool around. They just sit there."

I'd planned to stay quiet and let Adam handle his dad. I didn't want to get him in *more* trouble. But this was too much. "Adam's right," I piped up. "That's creep—"

"Can you believe this?" Adam interrupted me. He didn't care I was trying to back him up. He wasn't even listening. He turned to me and said, "You're a witness to this. It's probably the only time this has happened in the history of the United States. I'm in trouble for *not* doing you."

Mr. Vader took his hands off his hips and pointed at Adam's chest. "I won't have you talking like that in front of Lori. Or in front of *me*, for that matter." Which was ludicrous, because the boys had learned all their best figures of speech from Mr. Vader. So had I.

"Why not?" Adam's voice rose. "That's what you're talking about, right? And now you don't want to talk about it? Maybe you're sorry you brought it up. Maybe you see now that it's none of your business."

"It's my business when it's part of this stupid game between you and Sean."

"Which one?" I asked.

As if I hadn't spoken, Mr. Vader said to Adam, "Your mother was right. You and Lori aren't really dating. You're trying to make Rachel jealous and get her away from Sean."

Sean made Adam angry. I could only imagine what it was doing to Adam to find out his dad *bought* Sean's act. Adam was going to explode at his dad. He would be grounded. We wouldn't get to make Sean and Rachel jealous tonight. I put my arm around him and told Mr. Vader, "Maybe he's more of a gentleman than you think."

Adam gave me a look of utter disbelief. Despite how serious the situation was, I almost laughed.

He didn't explode, but his chest did expand, until I lost my hold around him. He turned back to Mr. Vader, held out his fingers, and touched the first one. "Sean." He touched his second finger and said, "Stole." He tapped his third finger vigorously. "*My.*" He touched his pinky. "Girlfriend."

Mr. Vader hmphed and half-turned away, finished with us. "It's obvious Sean has something good going on, as usual, and you're trying to ruin it. Sean bought Rachel a wakeboard. He gave it to her at dinner, in front of your mother and Cameron and me. You don't mess with something special like that." He stalked down the pier, toward the party.

Adam and I looked at each other. Sean had been saving the money he earned at the marina to buy a Byerly for himself. He'd bragged about it every day in the boat, like all he needed was this new trick wakeboard and he'd be numero uno again. We were talking hundreds of dollars.

He'd spent that money on Rachel instead?

Adam jogged down the pier and stepped in front of Mr. Vader, blocking his way. "What about bindings?"

"Bindings too," Mr. Vader said. "They're on order."

It didn't make sense for Mr. Vader to be proud of Sean buying his new girlfriend a wakeboard instead of buying one for himself. It was a frivolous purchase made way too soon in their relationship. Right? What Adam and I knew, and what Mr. Vader knew too but clearly wasn't admitting to himself, was that this was the first time Sean had ever done something selfless.

Or so it seemed. But he'd given it to her in front of his mom and dad, like he'd wanted to impress them more than her. The *ew* factor was off the charts. Parents were bad enough. You didn't go out of your way to *involve* them.

Adam was thinking the same thing. "Her birthday isn't until March. Why'd he make this big presentation at the dinner table?"

"Because he values her," Mr. Vader said haughtily, "and he wanted to show us how much he values her."

"Couldn't he value her out in the Volvo?" Adam hollered. "Jesus!"

Mr. Vader pushed past Adam and resumed his walk up the pier. Partygoers in his yard stepped out of his way. I watched him carve a swath through the crowd until he disappeared inside the house. I couldn't hear over the music, but I could tell from the way people near the house jerked their heads in that direction that Mr. Vader slammed the door.

Adam pinched his own arm thoughtfully. He reached over and pinched *my* arm.

"Ow!" I squeaked.

He took me by the shoulders and shook me gently. "He gave her a wakeboard."

"I know."

"In front of my parents. Because he values her." He imitated his dad's tone, heavy with gravity.

"*You* could have valued her," I pointed out. "You could have given her something that meant a lot to you." I nodded toward his neck.

His eyes flew wide open. He gripped the skull-and-crossbones pendant protectively. "*You* gave this to *me*."

We pinned each other with a long look, and I wished for the millionth time in the past week that I could read his mind. He was upset all over again about losing Rachel. He was mad at Sean about Rachel. He was outraged that his parents believed Sean over him about Rachel. But the pendant was more important to him than Rachel? Because I'd given it to him?

The boys with bottle rockets had noticed us and shouted to us. They were shooting bottle rockets near us in the water. Sooner or later they would set a boat on fire. Yet I couldn't tear my gaze away from Adam's blue eyes so bright in the gray mist. He must have seen something in my eyes, too.

"I'd better go change," I said slowly. "For the party."

"Right," Adam said, still holding my gaze.

"So." I laughed nervously. Dork. "I'll meet you back here in a while. Beauty takes patience. Ha ha ha ha."

He shook his head. "We should go to the party like this."

"Like *this*? My hair is full of lake."

"You look great in a bikini. As you know."

I was glad the dusk hid my blushing face. Or maybe it made my blushing face stand out like it made other colors pop, because I was that fortunate. "What do you mean, *as I know*? I don't *know*."

"If you didn't know, you wouldn't be wearing a bikini to get Sean's attention."

"Yeah. Fat lot of good it's done me."

"You wouldn't be flaunting it."

"*Flaunting* it! Are you sure? I have no idea what that would look like."

"Come flaunt it up at the house."

I wasn't sure why this irked me. He'd told me I looked good. He'd told me I would look good to Sean. This is what we wanted. Anyway, I couldn't stand out here and flaunt it for *anyone* in my bikini. I knew the night was hot and steamy, but the rain had done me in. I was freezing.

"Cold again?" he asked me, stepping closer.

I shivered some more. My stupid body had a mind of its own. "Toasty."

"Hold on." He took the extra key to the warehouse from the ledge above the door and stepped inside. He came back out with his zip-up sweatshirt printed with the name of our football team on the front and his number on the back. He held it up like an old man holding up an old lady's coat for her. I slipped my arms into the sleeves. Then he turned me around toward him. He pulled the hood up over my hair. Put the hood back down. Kissed me on the tip of my nose.

Foop! A bottle rocket exploded in the water just below us, illuminating a blob of bryozoa clinging to the wharf.

Adam took my hand, whispering, "We've got them right where we want them. Trust me."

He led me through the crowd in the yard, up the deck stairs, into his shadowy living room pulsing with music. Sean was surrounded by a group of people listening with open mouths to his puffed-up story of how he gave Rachel a wakeboard. Even Holly and Beige exclaimed like they were happy for Rachel instead of grumbling internally that Rachel was another in a long line and Sean was just showing off. Two feet away, Rachel was surrounded by hoydens screeching about how lucky she was to have a boyfriend like Sean.

From inside the dark room, the lights on the deck must have made Adam and me glow like a TV show. As we stepped through the door, everyone turned to stare at us.

I backed the slightest bit toward Adam. He squeezed my hand.

Then the floodgates opened. The girls who'd surrounded Rachel flocked to me to squeal about Adam spray-painting our names on the bridge. The boys with bottle rockets on the dock had seen it before the sun set and had spread the news around the party. The people who'd surrounded Sean moved to Adam and ribbed him about misspelling our names.

Adam played this perfectly. He laughed it all off like he didn't even care he was getting more attention than his stewing brother. He rubbed my shoulder and asked, "Aren't you hungry? We haven't eaten." He peered over my shoulder at the spread Mrs. Vader had laid out on the bar. "Party food isn't going to cover it."

"Starved." I followed him around the bar that divided the living room from the kitchen. There were partial walls on either side, so the kitchen was a little more quiet. At least we could raise our voices over the beat of Splender without making ourselves hoarse.

He opened the refrigerator door. "What'd they have for dinner? Chicken casserole." He wrinkled his nose. "I don't want the casserole of love, do you?"

"Definitely not."

"Hey, chica," Tammy called across the bar.

"Hey, chica," I responded, and looked

over Adam's shoulder into the refrigerator again. Then I realized what I was supposed to be doing. I walked around the bar, screamed, "Tammeeeee!" and hugged her while jumping up and down. This was a lot easier in bare feet than it had been in heels, let me tell you.

"Hi there," she said, wrestling me off her. "You're insane. I'm so late. My mom made me play in a stupid tennis tournament in Birmingham today. Where is everybody?" She peered into the kitchen.

"Don't I count?" Adam asked from inside the refrigerator.

"That's Adam, right?" Tammy whispered.

"Right," I said. "Sean is holding court by the palm tree in the living room. The art geeks are outside in the grass."

"The football team is on the dock, shooting bottle rockets into the lake," Adam offered. I knew where his heart was.

"The trumpet line from the marching band is on the deck," I said. "Who were you looking for?"

"You!" Tammy said. She handed me a small present wrapped in Valentine's paper.

"Hey, thanks!" I said, ripping it open.

"What's it for?" My birthday was still a week and a day away, and I didn't think anyone from school knew when it was. "How sweet!" I held up the eyelash comb, twirled it between my fingers, and slipped it into the pocket of Adam's sweatshirt. I hoped I remembered to take it out again at the end of the night. If I didn't, Adam would have some explaining to do next football season when it fell out of his pocket at practice.

"It's a hostess gift," Tammy said. "You know, when you come to a party, you bring a present for the hostess."

"But I'm not the hostess. This isn't my house." I wondered whether she'd tripped over some tennis balls, hit her head, and forgotten she'd gone with me to my house last week, scaring the bejeezus out of the father figure.

"You're the hostess because you're the girlfriend of one of the hosts," Tammy said.

Without meaning to, I glanced up at Adam. He'd closed the refrigerator door and leaned against it, watching me.

"Or *pretending* to be," Tammy added.

Adam's blue eyes widened at me. Something told me—and I am sure this was not feminine instincts, because we have established I did not have any of those—but *something* told me my explanation of how Tammy knew about the plot might go over better if I heated Adam up. I slid my arms around his waist and pressed close to him, backing him against the refrigerator. His eyes grew even wider.

I gave him a coy half-smile that probably ended up looking like the first signs of a seizure. "You know how girls are. Girls can't make a move without telling other girls about it."

"Yeah, *girls* are like that," Adam told me, "but *you're* not."

Tammy cleared her throat.

Adam cleared his throat.

I cleared my throat, removed my hands from Adam's waist, and brushed imaginary dust off his bare shoulders, setting straight any oafish damage I might have done. From now on, whenever I got the idea that maybe he liked me a little, I would remember that he did *not* like me a little. I didn't need to read his mind.

"Heeeeeeey," Tammy squealed. She must have seen Holly or Beige or a super-cute boy—but no, it was only McGillicuddy. They disappeared into the living room with their heads close together, shouting over the music. If she got rid of my approaching brother for me because she thought I needed some alone time with Adam to talk out our problems, she was wrong-o about me. Again. I started to follow her.

"Dinner's ready," Adam said behind me.

I looked toward the table in the kitchen. He'd set two of the places with knives, forks, spoons, and napkins. He'd placed a sandwich on each plate and sprinkled parsley flakes in a circle around it. Bam! He'd stacked the potato chips artfully in dessert bowls. He'd even lit one of his leftover birthday candles between our places. It all would have been really cute if he'd meant it. It was still pretty cute as a farce to make Rachel jealous, I supposed, but I wasn't in the mood.

"Let me help you," he said, pulling out a chair for me, as if I were a girl or something. Vivid imagination, this boy. I sat, and he scooted me up to the table.

He took a bottle of soda from the fridge and held it in front of me, like he was a wine steward. I nodded that the year was okay. He unscrewed the cap and handed it to me.

I sniffed it like a wine cork, nodded my approval again, and handed it back to him. He poured soda into wine glasses for both of us, then sat down with me.

He took a gargantuan bite of his sandwich, chewed, swallowed, and looked at me. "What's wrong?"

Oh, nothing. That's what a girl would say, and she'd sulk for the rest of the night. But I wasn't capable of keeping my mouth shut. "I'm confused."

"It's not really wine," he said. "It's Diet Coke. And if anyone *ever* serves you brown wine with a foamy head, send it back."

"Thank you, Dr. Science." I took a dainty bite of my sandwich. Adam was a real gourmet. Peanut butter and strawberry jam. "I'm confused because I thought you said I was flaunting, and now I'm not even a girl? I thought you said I was a good flaunter."

"You *are* a good flaunter." He swirled the Diet Coke in his glass and sniffed the bouquet.

"Then why am I not a girl?"

"You— Shit, I *knew* that's what you were mad about. I didn't mean it that way." He leaned his head to one side and popped his neck. "You know as well as I do that you don't act like other girls."

"I'm working on it, though." I was working so hard! I felt like crying into my salt and vinegar chips, which was a step in the right direction.

"But it's *good* you don't act like other girls. Of course, I don't have any say in it, because you're not after me. You're after Sean."

"You wouldn't have any *say* in it *anyway*, you patriarchal freak." I chomped a chip and said with my mouth full, "Thanks for cooking dinner. I love it when the little missus makes a house a home."

He glared at me. "Eat up. We have work to do."

"What kind of work? Devious kissing work? May I point out that we both have peanut butter breath?"

"Eat up," he said again. Sean's jovial voice escalated over the music in the living room, which made me want to speed up eating to get out of there, but also made the sandwich sit on my stomach like a rock.

We went upstairs. Adam shared his bathroom with Sean and Cameron, and the bathroom looked it. He brushed his teeth, then sipped straight from a bottle of mouthwash. As he swished it around in his mouth, he nudged my bare tummy with his toothbrush and prompted, "Hm."

"You want me to *use your toothbrush?*"

He spit in the sink. "You might as well. You're about to do a lot worse."

Fourteen

At this point, I realized what I'd thought was stress and peanut butter indigestion was actually butterflies, which began dog-fighting in my stomach at the idea that Adam and I were about to kiss some more. As I brushed my teeth with his tooth-brush, I watched him watching me in the mirror. His muscled arms were folded on his strong, tanned chest. The bruise Sean had given him under his eye had almost faded, but the skull-and-crossbones pendant glinted dangerously.

If his parents hadn't been in the next room with the ten o'clock news turned way up over the music downstairs, I might have made a move on him right there in the bathroom.

Yes, I know, odds were I would have tripped and knocked him down and made him hit his head on the toilet. I was so turned on, I was almost willing to take this chance.

Instead, he took my hand again and led me down through the party, indoors and outdoors, to the end of the dock. The football team had run out of bottle rockets. The party had reached the stage where boys played quarters. The drinking game was run very professionally by experienced people. If Mr. Vader had found out, he would have shut down the party—because kids were drinking underage at his house, or because he would have known one of his sons had stolen beer from the marina. In any case, as a precaution, a wall of people stood across the dock, talking and flirting, shielding the boys playing quarters from the prying eyes of the Vaders in their bedroom.

The wall of people included Sean and Rachel, facing each other and holding both hands like they were about to dance a polka. Rachel hadn't taken the precaution of kicking her shoes off before she stepped onto the dock. She was likely to catch her heel between the boards and fall flat. (Shrug.) Rachel obviously valued beauty before balance.

As Adam and I approached the wall of people, Adam aimed straight for Sean. He brushed against Sean harder than necessary as we edged through. I felt Sean and Rachel watching us, but I didn't look back as we stepped over the boys sprawled in a circle around a cup of beer.

We sat on the edge of the dock. The wood was still damp and cold from the rain. We slipped our feet into the lake, which felt like a warm bath compared with the cool air.

"Do you want a beer?" Adam asked.

"I don't think I could handle it. I feel so high already." The warm lake, the cool air, and Adam had my body going in a thousand different directions.

Maybe he knew. He grinned at me and whispered, "I'm going to kiss you now. It'll be a big one, so don't hit me." He leaned in.

"Wait a minute," I said, putting my hand on his chest to stop him. I wasn't quite ready to kiss him with boys playing quarters right behind us, and with Sean and Rachel staring at us. We'd kissed before where people could see us if they wanted to look, but we'd never been this blatant about it. Besides, I had another concern. "I want to be prepared. Are you going to kiss me, or *really* kiss me?"

He cocked his head at me, perplexed, with those little frown lines between his eyebrows. "What would be the point of kissing you if I didn't do it right?"

"Ohhhhhh!" said the boys behind us. There was nowhere in my life I could get away from boys saying, "Ohhhhhh!" I glanced behind us to make sure the boys were talking about beer, not us. Indeed, when the boys' quarters hit the cup and they chose someone to drink, all of them seemed to be ganging up on Scooter Ledbetter. I hadn't seen his monster truck in the Vaders' driveway, so at least he wouldn't be driving home.

Sean had moved Rachel in front of him and held her with his arms crossed over her boobs. So he could watch us over her head without her knowing. Of course, she was staring at Adam, too. I rolled my eyes at both of them, like I was *so tired* of them watching us. I almost burst into laughter at the thought, but managed to turn back to Adam in time.

I told him through my teeth, "We've been kissing all week without, you know. *Really* kissing."

"That was before Sean gave up a wakeboard for Rachel. Step up your game."

I was running out of excuses. "Look," I whispered, "when we do this stuff, we're trying to make them jealous, but it's also my first time for real. You know?"

His blue eyes focused on me. We were almost nose to nose, and our shoulders moved quickly in time with our breathing, in time with each other. "I know."

"And when I fantasize about kissing"—kissing Sean, I meant, but I wasn't going to say this—"our mouths are closed."

"This isn't your fantasy."

I wasn't so sure about that. True, I'd never fantasized about this particular scenario, but maybe that was because I'd never imagined it. I had to remember that this was *Adam Adam Adam*, and if I could replace him with Sean from my fantasies, the warm pricklies I was feeling would make a perfect dream. Except I would probably wake up.

Adam moved in again. One more time my brain knew this would make Sean jealous, but my body sounded the alarm. I put my hand on Adam's chest and whispered, "Give me a break. I had a bad experience with this."

He looked hurt, which didn't make sense if we were only friends. He was putting on a good act. "With who?"

"The only person I've ever kissed, besides you, is Cameron."

"You kissed *Ca—*"

I hadn't expected his reaction to be that LOUD. I reached out and grabbed the back of his hair, which turned his head away from the crowd and also shut him up right quick.

I put my forehead to his forehead and whispered like a lover, "I was eleven. We were in the warehouse and he grabbed me. Very sloppy. Don't tell McGillicuddy."

Adam blinked. I felt his eyelashes on my eyelids.

"Very, very sloppy," I said. "We still can't look each other in the eye."

I let go of his hair so he could look *me* in the eye. "Let me shrug that off." He shook violently like he'd caught a sudden chill. "Okay. I'm going to *really* kiss you, but it'll be subtle." He moved toward me one more time. "And don't tell me to back off. It's starting to look like we're not really in love."

I closed my eyes automatically as he kissed me, and the word *love* blinked red and then black on the insides of my eyelids. His lips were warm. Was that all? I opened my eyes.

His eyes were still closed, and he came in again.

I closed my eyes. He kissed me like before, only I felt his tongue between my lips, opening them. His tongue was inside my mouth (ADAM VADER'S TONGUE WAS INSIDE MY MOUTH) not very far, and then out again.

I thought *that* was it, and opened my eyes. And closed them as he kissed me once more. Now I was getting it. You didn't just sit there with your lips locked with the boy's lips and the boy's tongue turning flips at the back of your throat (cough *Cameron* cough). There was constant movement and change. It was an activity, and probably one the girl could participate in, too. As Adam pulled away, I said, "Let me try."

He kissed me and whispered against my lips, "Be my guest." His low voice made me shiver.

I kissed him. Strange that the lips were so soft in such an edgy boy. I kissed him again and very gently pressed my tongue into his mouth.

He gasped. I mean, I wasn't sure, because it was in the middle of the kiss. But he seemed startled. He inhaled sharply through his nose. Then *he* was kissing *me*, deeper this time.

I pulled away, laughing. "It was supposed to be my turn."

He half-smiled. His lips stayed close to my lips.

I didn't suggest this, and he didn't agree to this, but somehow we telepathically agreed to give up on the witty conversation and make out. His tongue played with my lips. My tongue swept across his teeth. I drowned in it, and completely lost the people playing quarters behind us on the dock until someone said, "Is anybody filming Adam and Lori? You might be able to sell it." Sean laughed and said something I couldn't catch that made the people around him burst into laughter too.

Adam pulled back. He was embarrassed and saw our plan wasn't working. He would escape to his room, humiliated. He would leave me naked, or nearly so, in my bikini and his sweatshirt in the midst of these fully clothed people.

Wrong. He kissed me again and whispered, "There's something else you can do if you get bored with this."

Get *bored* with this???

"You kind of do the same thing, but move around. Here." He kissed my jaw. His tongue touched my skin just as he pulled his lips away. "Or up here." Good Lord, his teeth were on my earlobe. Very gently he slid them off. His tongue played outside my ear. His breath was loud and hot.

It felt so good, and at the same time, I could hardly stand it. I needed something to hang onto. My fingers patted the edge of the dock, finding a firm hold—but this seemed potentially splintery. My other hand felt for Adam's hand.

Strangely, he must have needed something to hang onto, too. He took my hand and squeezed.

The guys playing quarters may have made another comment about us, but it was hard to hear with a boy's tongue in my ear. Also it was hard to care.

I pulled away, shoulders shaking. Adam seemed to have a hard time focusing his eyes on me, like he was in a dream. I moved in and gave him the jaw treatment. Then the ear treatment.

"Ah," he said. He giggled and then cleared his throat before the boys heard him. "Lori."

"Mm?" I hummed in his ear.

He shuddered. And then—oh, no! He stood up. I'd done something wrong! The tongue was indeed el grosso as I'd originally thought!

"I'll be right back," he told me. He picked his way across the quarters game and pushed through the wall of people watching. He had sense enough not to push through Sean and Rachel again, or they'd know the ear was for them. At least, they'd *think* the ear was for them. I was beginning to wonder who the ear was for. It *felt* like it was for me.

He came back dragging a beanbag float and nearly knocked the legs out from under a few folks. He dragged it right over the quarters game, scattering the boys, and would have spilled the beer if someone hadn't been faster. Then he dropped the float into the lake and kicked off the part of it that sagged over the dock. He gestured toward it and grinned at me. "Your limo awaits."

I had my doubts about this. The lake was black, and the sky was black with far-away stars. But anyone who drove their boat to the party this late would know to dock at the marina where there was more room. We were safe. I shrugged off Adam's sweatshirt and—*without looking to see if Sean was watching me*, very important—slipped into the hot water. I hadn't realized my butt was frozen solid from the cold dock. The lake was such a relief. Ahhhhh.

Until Adam did a cannonball, socking me in the eyes with water and splashing everyone on the dock, including Sean and Rachel.

"Aaaadaaaaaaaam!" they all cried. He chuckled softly to himself as we held onto the raft and kicked it out into the lake, beyond the glow of light from the house.

He stopped kicking and crawled higher on the raft, straddling it. "Come up here with me."

The beanbag raft was filled with floaty bits rather than air and always seemed in danger of sinking. This could be annoying when you wanted to stay on top of the water, getting a tan. On a night like tonight, it was perfect. It would keep us from drowning while giving us more hot water than cool air.

"Now. Where were we?" He put both

his strong arms around me, pulled me close, and kissed me hard.

I hadn't thought this was possible, but it was even better than before, because no one was watching. Which was actually my new problem with it. I put my hand on his chest to stop him.

He groaned in frustration. I made a mental note to make him groan in frustration more often. It seemed like something a treacherous girl would do. Also he was really cute when he groaned.

"I just wanted to know," I breathed, "why we're doing this where no one can see us."

"We think no one can. We thought no one was watching us at the bridge. We need to act the part all the time, and never step out of character." He put his hand on my arm. "If that's okay."

I nodded. I was still nodding as he pushed me gently backward until I was lying down on the raft, and he was lying on top of me. His whole weight was on me, but he didn't squash me because I was hovering on the raft, just under the surface of the warm water. I felt him along me. Almost every inch of his skin touched almost every inch of mine.

I watched the skull and crossbones glinting in the starlight, and tried to impress it on my retinas so I'd still see it when I closed my eyes to kiss him again. This was Adam, not Sean. I was after Sean, not Adam. Adam was after Rachel, not me. And if kissing Adam was better than anything I'd ever dreamed of doing with Sean . . . well, I could see how that was going to mess up my plans.

I kissed him anyway. The skull and crossbones lay on my throat.

"And when you kiss me," I said against his lips, "you're thinking about Rachel. Right?"

Almost before I got the last word out, he was kissing me again, harder than before, so intense I got lost in it and thought I might drown in the blackness even though my head was still above water.

I pinched his ass.

He yelped, and the yelp echoed across the lake and back. Silhouettes moved far away on the dock, peering in our direction without seeing.

"Did you hear me?" I asked.

He propped himself far enough above me to be able to see me. With one finger he smoothed a strand of wet hair away from my face. He traced the line of my cheek down to my chin. "Do you want to stop? Tell me and I'll stop."

"I don't want to stop," I said. The absolute truth, for the first time in a week. "But how far are we going with this?" Adam was used to jumping off the roof. I wasn't. These were dangerous waters.

He moved to my ear again, and my body braced for the shockwaves. Just before his lips touched my skin, he whispered, "I guess we'll know when we get there."

Fifteen

"S-bend or what?" Adam asked me, grinning.

I'd just climbed out of the water after *landing the S-bend*! And even though he'd dried in the hot sun and hugging me must have been a cold, wet shock, he wrapped his strong arms around my life vest and hugged me hard. Best of all, Adam acting this way wasn't an unexpected hostess gift wrapped in Valentine's paper anymore. It was part of being his girlfriend. I was getting used to it, and I *loved* expecting it.

Saturday we'd gone mud riding. Then we'd parked in the movie theater lot, watched the trucks go by, and just talked. We'd shared a milkshake. I was totally immune to his germs by now. Monday after dinner, when I thought I'd have to spend the evening with Arthur C. Clarke, who wrote a good space story but was not the greatest kisser, Adam asked me to go for a walk around the neighborhood with him. We held hands, which no longer seemed the least bit weird. Here it was Wednesday, and I hadn't had more than a fleeting thought of Sean since Friday night with Adam in the lake.

I could have sworn Adam hadn't thought of Rachel, either. When he kissed me (often! *really* kissed me!), it felt like he was thinking of *me*, not her. Yeah, he could have been faking. But as he'd said that first night at the tennis court, he wasn't exactly drama club material.

And it would come crashing down around us any minute. Adam never looked over his shoulder to make sure Rachel was watching us when he kissed. He *did* check *Sean's* reaction. I knew Mr. Vader was wrong about which of his boys was stabbing the other in the back, but I also knew Adam wouldn't walk away after being stabbed, any more than Sean would. So I enjoyed my time alone with Adam as much as I could. Whenever Sean came around, I held my breath, waiting for the fall.

It wasn't so long a wait. The boys *looked* harmless enough this afternoon. Adam, Cameron and my brother had had fantastic wakeboarding runs, too. They'd finally gotten their wakeboarding legs back, as good as last year. Cameron and McGillicuddy lounged across the seats in the boat, basking in the late afternoon sunshine like big golden retrievers, watching me drip on the platform and wagging their tails vaguely. They felt what I'd been feeling since the first day we went out: sated with happy exertion. High.

Sean lay flattened across the bow seat, but not for the same reason. He hadn't taken his turn yet. He said he didn't want to miss a call from Rachel. She'd planned to come wakeboarding with us today (amid protests from the boys, because guests had never been allowed) and borrow my wakeboard since her bindings hadn't arrived yet (whatever). Her mom was going to bring her down, but they never showed. Sean had called Rachel four times from the boat (to make Adam mad, Adam and I thought) and hadn't reached her. I found this strange. Where was she? Wasn't she waiting around for Sean's call with her hand poised on the answer button of her phone?

Beyond the windshield that separated us from him, we heard his cell phone ring Nickelback's "Fight for All the Wrong Reasons." We knew it was Rachel calling him back. And when his curse word burst over the windshield, we knew what she'd said hadn't been very nice.

Adam shrugged and turned back to me. Unlike Sean, he didn't flirt with me by assisting me with things I was perfectly capable of doing myself. He didn't help me off with my equipment. He did sit on the back of the boat and watch me appreciatively. When I took off my life vest, he surveyed my bikini-clad hotness (ha) and gave me a naughty smile. I untied my bindings and lifted one foot out. He licked his lips like he had a foot fetish. I burst into laughter.

Sean charged past the windshield into the back of the boat, eyes full of tears. "She broke up with me!" he wailed. "She broke up with me because she's still in love with Adam!"

We all went quiet. Only the *clack-clack, clack-clack* of cars on the bridge and the lapping of waves against the boat disturbed the silence. The boys weren't ribbing Sean. They must have been as shocked as I was that Sean would *admit* what Rachel had said.

Sean was in love.

He sniffled. "I'm going to her house. Take me back to shore." When Cameron didn't immediately slip into the driver's seat, Sean took a step toward the steering wheel himself.

"Sean," Cameron said, standing in his way. "You haven't landed a good trick the whole week and a half we've been coming out. We only have today, tomorrow and Friday to practice for the Crappy Festival. Take your turn first and then go to her house."

Sean cursed, and cursed, and cursed, and dove into the lake. We all rushed to the side of the boat and watched him glide to the surface twenty feet away, already swimming. We weren't so far from the Foshees' yard that we needed to fish him out for his own safety. He swam until he could touch bottom, sloshed the rest of the way to land, and hit the grass running through the Foshees' yard, through my yard, toward his house.

Adam said quietly, "I'm the biggest."

"Adam," I scolded him.

Cameron and my brother looked from me to Adam and back to me, wondering what was going on between us. Frankly, I wondered the same thing. I wasn't sure what I'd wanted or expected Adam to say when we finally got our wish for Sean and Rachel to break up. But *I'm the biggest* wasn't it.

We drove back to the wharf still in silence—except, of course, for the deafening motor. Adam and I sat across the aisle from each other without glancing at each other. Something was about to happen.

And everyone sensed it. Cameron and McGillicuddy took more than their share of equipment into the warehouse, leaving Adam and me alone in the boat. As they came back out, Cameron looked down at us from the wharf and said, "Don't do anything I wouldn't do"—which made me wish I hadn't confessed to Adam that Cameron and I had kissed. After five years of hiding this from everyone, he had to hint about it *now*? Whatever was coming for Adam and me, it was going to be hard enough already.

McGillicuddy asked me, "Do you want me to tell Dad you'll be late for dinner?"

"No," I said. "I won't be long."

We watched McGillicuddy and Cameron walk toward the houses. They stopped to talk. Cameron took a swipe at McGillicuddy. McGillicuddy shoved Cameron. They went their separate ways. Friends to the end, the simplest relationship possible.

"What's that supposed to mean?" Adam snapped into the silence. "You won't be long?"

"It's dusk in the summer. Mosquitos," I said, slapping at a bug. While my mouth spouted this drivel, my mind worked on what I really wanted to say to Adam. But I had no more idea than I'd had out on the lake.

You know what didn't help? When he reached behind his neck and worked at the knot in the leather string. I knew what was coming. It took him a few seconds to get through that knot. Even though the whole time I was thinking about what to say when he asked me to turn around, I was speechless when the moment came. I turned around on my seat. He tied the skull and crossbones around my neck. The metal was hot against my breastbone. I pressed the skull between the eyes with my fingertips. Turning back to him, I murmured, "You're giving me a piece of you."

He looked over at me. We were together

for real, and he was *so hot*. I should have been giggling with delight and dorkiness. The angry look in his blue eyes broke my heart.

"Rachel told Sean she likes you better," I said, "but you don't want her back. You've never wanted her back. All you've wanted was to get revenge on Sean. You're giving me this to show him you don't even want what he can't have."

Adam's eyes narrowed at me. I made an effort not to shrink back against the side of the boat. He said evenly, "I'm giving it to you because I want to give it to you."

"Your timing is odd. Usually a boy wouldn't laugh at his brother hitting rock bottom, then show his love for his girlfriend practically in the same breath." Now *he* was shrinking against his side of the boat, which made me brave enough to throw in still more sarcasm. "I don't have a lot of experience with this, but that's my theory."

He closed his eyes and said in a rush, "I'm in love with you."

I took a breath to tell him if he really meant it, he wouldn't have to say it with his eyes closed. But he didn't just have his eyes closed. Those worry lines had appeared between his brows. He was in pain, concentrating hard to make it go away, like the second time he broke his collarbone wakeboarding, and lay still as death in the floorboard of the boat and wouldn't let anyone touch him but me.

He opened his eyes but remained plastered against the boat. He looked small, if this was possible. "That's my plot. You were right, I had a plot, and that's my whole plot. I'm in love with you. The last nine months with McGillicuddy away at college have been freaking torture for me, because I didn't have an excuse to come to your house. If I came over without McGillicuddy there, you'd know. I hardly saw you the whole school year. I thought I might finally have a chance with you since I was about to get my license, and you were about to get your license. We could go places together, alone. I could get you away from Sean. But the more I hinted we should go out, the more you talked about hooking up with Sean. When I heard Rachel liked me, I asked her out, and I kept asking her out. To make you jealous. And at the tennis court that night when you said we should make Rachel and Sean jealous, I nearly had a heart attack. I thought you saw right through me."

He looked so hurt, and his eyelashes were so long. I had fallen in love with him. I *wished* he were in love with me too. But in telling me this elaborate lie, he'd betrayed the truth.

"You don't love me," I said. "You're competing with Sean. Maybe you've even convinced yourself you love me, but it all comes back to Sean."

His expression changed from hurt back to anger. "Last Friday night in the lake didn't mean anything to you."

Friday night had been the best night of my life. He was picking up each thing I loved about my life, grinding it to a point, and pushing it through my heart. I'd thought only Sean knew how to do that.

"The past week and a half hasn't meant anything to you," he went on. "The past sixteen years—"

"Sixteen years!" I howled.

"You *told* me you're stuck on Sean," he shouted. His voice made the metal wall of the warehouse hum. "You think your mother chose him for you—"

"No, I don't!" Well, maybe I did. And maybe I didn't care so much anymore, but this was hard to explain while yelling.

"Look, Adam. Let's say you *had* been in love with me all our lives, which, by the way, I don't believe for a second." Because why would any boy fall in love with a girl like me? "What you loved about me would have been exactly what I hate about myself. To stay the person you wanted, I'd have to stay the same. I want to change."

"You think your *mother* wants you to change," he corrected me. "Lori, when your mother said that, she was kidding."

"You weren't there. You don't know. *Your* mother didn't laugh."

"My mother *never* laughs. It's called a dry wit. You're basing your whole life on one conversation you overheard when you were four years old that you don't even remember right."

I felt like I'd been slapped. When I'd shared my deepest secret with him, it never once occurred to me that he'd throw it back in my face. Adam, of all people, had betrayed me. I stepped out of the boat, onto the wharf. "Let's end this now before we ruin our friendship."

"Too late," he called after me.

I intended to flounce across his yard and mine, but I ran straight into a cloud of gnats. I spent the rest of the walk pressing one nostril closed with my finger while I expelled gnats from the other. Eat your heart out, Adam!

Except I *didn't* want him to eat his heart out. I wanted to be friends with him. I wanted to be with him. I wanted to make out with him in the lake some more—that was for damn sure. I wanted him to stare longingly after me from the boat as I flounced to my house, which sounded a lot like I wanted him to eat his heart out. I didn't know what I wanted.

I'd made it to my garage before I realized I was still wearing the skull and crossbones. I couldn't get the knot undone. I turned the knot around to the front but still couldn't pick it apart. The pendant was searing a hole through my skin. I cut through the leather string with garden shears and tried to grind the pendant into dust in my fist like a superhero. I opened my hand and found the outline of the skull and crossbones pressed into my palm.

I didn't sleep well that night. This was probably a good thing. If I'd had to lie through one more dream about Sean being a tease, I would have had to slap him. When I woke up and found myself sleepwalking, who knew what wakeboarding posters I might have destroyed? I might even have found myself choking my childhood teddy bear, Mr. Wuggles, which would have traumatized me for life.

In the morning, I walked to the marina with the skull and crossbones in my pocket (actually, Adam's pocket, the pocket of his cutoff jeans), intending to give it back to him and say something appropriate. This would have been a stretch for me, I know. To save my friendship with Adam, I would have found a way to do it.

Mrs. Vader assigned us both to the warehouse. Great, *now* she finally believed we were together? I tried to look at the long day with him as an opportunity to have a heart-to-heart with him. Another one. Actually the convo the evening before had been more of a spleen-to-spleen.

I could never find the right time. He was busy locating boats to take down. I was busy checking the oil. The full-time workers wandered in and out. Besides, this day of all days, he worked with his shirt off. Sweat glistened on his tanned muscles, and his brown hair fell in his eyes. He was so hot that I felt intimidated. He was telling me to eat *my* heart out, and it was working.

There were a few instances when I *could* have screwed up my courage, sidled up to him, handed him the skull and crossbones, and talked him down. But whenever I started toward him with this in mind, he flashed those blue eyes at me, and I felt that slap all over again.

It was such a relief to go wakeboarding that afternoon. Yes, I'd be trapped in the boat for over an hour with Adam and Sean, but at least I was out of the warehouse and into the strong sun and oppressive humidity. The Crappy Festival show was in two days. We all needed to nail down the course we wanted the boat to follow and the tricks we planned to do—especially Sean. Maybe thinking about the show would get our minds off each other.

Or not. Adam climbed out of the water and onto the platform after busting ass four times. He had a stare-down with Sean, who was getting in the water for his turn. If two girls had been in a fight like this, one of them would have flipped over the side of the boat rather than face probably the tenth stare-down of the day. But Sean and Adam were not two girls. And because *I* was a girl, it stressed me out more to watch them than it stressed them to growl at each other, teeth bared. I left my seat and slid into the bow, watching ahead of us as the boat drifted across the choppy water kicked up by the afternoon traffic.

The bench sank next to me, pulling me down into the hole. "So you still want Sean?" Adam hissed. "Let me give you some advice."

"No thanks." I leaned further over the bow to watch the large waves. A whitecap rolled by. A *whitecap*? You didn't see those on the lake very often. The water was choppier than I'd ever seen it.

"At first," Adam went on, "we thought we'd make him want something I had. You. Now he wants something *you* have."

"Boobs?" I asked, trying to sound bored.

"Your place at the end of the wakeboarding show. Throw a jump and fake an injury. You have to make it look like you're really hurt, so Cameron doesn't rib Sean about girls making sacrifices just to go out with him."

Cameron cranked the boat to pull Sean

up, and my brother spotted. With the motor roaring and Nickelback blaring, I was free to tell Adam (loudly) exactly what I thought of that plan. I sat up and turned to face him.

Before I could get the words out, he leaned close and said, "I told you before you're not a good actress. I have a lot more confidence in you now. I thought you liked me. You had me fooled."

I stared into his blue eyes, trying to see what was behind them. "You really want me to throw a jump and go out with Sean?"

"This has nothing to do with me," he said grimly.

"It has everything to do with y—"

He put his finger to my lips. "If you want Sean, this is what you need to do, because this is how he is. Love him or leave him. I'm just trying to help." He slid off the seat with a high zipping sound of his board shorts against the vinyl and bounced toward the back of the boat. He plopped down in the seat across the aisle from my brother and crossed his feet on the edge of the boat, relaxed, satisfied by a job well done. When Sean landed a front flip, then tumbled a couple of extra times before face-planting, Adam's shoulders shook. He was laughing.

"Lori!" McGillicuddy shouted, standing directly in front of me. The boat drifted again, and Sean dripped on the platform. "I said, did you see the log? I guess you didn't see the log, since you're in a coma."

"Log schmog." I stood up and reached for my life vest.

McGillicuddy followed me as I stepped over Adam and Sean, who didn't bother to move their feet out of the aisle as I passed. Just like old times. "There's a huge log out near the pontoon boat," McGillicuddy said. "When we get near it, I'm veering to the right of where we usually go. Okay?"

"Okay," I said, sliding over the back of the boat to the platform and stepping into the bindings on my wakeboard.

"To the *right*," Cameron laughed.

"I said *okay*." I was in no mood to be teased about my driving right now.

The drone of the motorboat was great for thinking, fortunately, or unfortunately, depending on whether you hated yourself. At the moment I wasn't enjoying it too much. I was supposed to be pinning down my routine for the show, but I just did flips and 360s automatically, my mind on Adam.

Staring at him in the boat told me nothing. He was so far away that he was just a tan face with light brown hair, and if he'd changed places with Sean, I wouldn't have known. But I stared at the boy I thought was Adam and tried to figure out exactly what he was plotting. Clearly he'd paid more attention to *Laguna Beach* than he'd let on.

If I pretended to get hurt so Sean could take my place in the show, he probably wouldn't ask me out. He'd watched Adam and me while we were together, that was for sure. And I'd thought at first that the light had dawned and he'd seen my ravishing beauty for the first time. Looking back, though, I thought he'd watched Adam more than me. Sean had worried Rachel would get jealous and Adam would snatch her away again.

If Sean *did* ask me out, though, I'd know for sure that my internal makeover had worked—two days before the deadline of my sixteenth birthday! And I'd also know Adam had been right. Sean was so low, he couldn't stand to ask out a girl who'd shown him up. It was almost worth throwing a jump just to see what happened and get some closure on this issue.

I could do any old jump and pretend to hurt my ankle. I'd hurt it last summer when I fell and my foot came halfway out of the binding, which was why I'd laced up the bindings so tightly since then. Faking a limp would be more difficult. But I'd need to limp for only two days, until the Crappy Festival show. The question was whether I should complain about it enough to go to the hospital and have them find nothing, which seemed like a huge waste of time and money. Adam had hurt himself before and had been in a lot of pain but refused to go to the hospital, so there *was* some precedent for this. Of course, he finally had to go, and his arm was broken in three places. There was also the small detail that Adam was like that and I was not.

Suddenly I found myself shooting farther and faster beyond the boat than I'd expected. We were turning at the bridge, just under the words AOAN LOVES LOKI. I pulled up and took control of the run.

What had I been thinking? Had I seriously been considering throwing a jump and pretending to be hurt just to get a boy? What kind of boy did you catch with a ploy like that?

And furthermore, what kind of person was Adam to give me the idea?

I decided right then that I was *not* going to pretend to get hurt and throw this show for Sean or anybody. *Furthermore*, I would skip the party tomorrow night, because there would be no one there I wanted to see, except Tammy. Well, okay, maybe I wouldn't skip the party, because who could skip a party next door? But I wouldn't enjoy it. Or I would hang out with Tammy, ignoring the boys. And *furthermore*, sometime between now and then, maybe tonight since I obviously would not have a boy to go out with, I would ask McGillicuddy to drive me to town. I would buy the latest Kelly Clarkson album as a birthday present from me to me. I would fight and fight and fight to play it in the boat the next time we went wakeboarding. I was sick to death of Nickelback.

Something dark in the water flashed past the corner of my eye. I turned and saw an enormous log tumbling gently in the water. Just then the pull on the rope changed, and I remembered McGillicuddy was veering to the right to avoid the log. I veered to the right with him as I headed for the pontoon boat to ride the rails.

Only I was coming up too fast on the backside of the pontoon boat. I glanced over at the boys and motioned to Adam to slow down. I'd screwed this trick already.

Adam was motioning to *me*, an exaggerated wave away from the pontoon boat. And he was mouthing something. *Your other right*. I realized what I'd done then and dropped the rope. The side of the pontoon boat emblazoned VADER'S MARINA zoomed toward me, *smack*.

Sixteen

This probably would have been a lot easier if I'd gotten amnesia or at least felt a little woozy from the impact, but I didn't. I knew exactly what was happening as I slipped wakeboard-first under the pontoon boat and slowed to a stop. The buoyant wakeboard on my feet and the life vest hugging my chest stuck me like magnets to the slippery underside of the boat.

My head—I had cracked my head open when I hit the boat, and the pain was almost unbearable, but I had nowhere to put it. Blood curled around me, backlit by sunbeams streaming through the water at the edges of the boat. I needed to get out from under. I was running out of air.

I tried to kick myself over to the edge—but my feet were still stuck in the wakeboard bindings. Bending over to untie them was the only way out. I would run out of air before then. I could hardly think of anything except running out of air, the throbbing in my head, the blood forming graceful curlicues in front of my eyes.

I reached one hand as far toward the edge of the boat as I could, hoping I could pull hard with every bit of life I had left and slip out from under, dragging the wakeboard with me. My hand sank into a firm, gelatinous mass. Without looking, I knew it was bryozoa. I had died and gone to hell. This was how my mother must have felt. The water had always been my friend. The water had betrayed me.

Then they came for me. They were under the pontoon boat with me, blurry and green like ghosts in the water. One boy shoved down on the wakeboard. The other boy put a strong arm across my chest and pushed off from the bottom of the boat with his feet. He took me lower in the water—wrong direction, hello, I could hardly suppress the urge to breathe in water instead of air. I struggled. He let me go. The wakeboard and the life vest propelled me to the surface, clear of the boat.

I popped into the air, gasping. Sean put his arms around me again and held my head above the water so I could breathe. The thought crossed my mind of rejecting a boy's help and resisting the damsel-in-distress role, but really it was a little thought that had no effect on letting Sean help me breathe. The more I breathed, the harder my head throbbed, so I also had a little thought that MTV would never invite me to dance on stage during one of their Spring Break specials now that I looked like the Elephant Man.

And a little thought that I had been wrong about Sean. Mom had sent me a sign. She'd sent Sean to save my life. Maybe he *was* worth a faked injury, after all.

Of course, there was also McGillicuddy down at my feet, and the fact that the motorboat had been only twenty yards away from me when I went down, so maybe it wasn't Mom's doing. God, my head hurt like a mother.

McGillicuddy got me loose from the wakeboard. Sean held me up to Cameron in the boat, who grabbed me under the arms and lifted me in. Immediately Sean climbed the ladder and came to me. He pulled me out of the life vest, then eased me down and cradled my head in his lap.

Just like in my dream, he looked down at me with eyes lighter than the deep blue sky behind him. The sunlight turned his hair and shoulders and broad chest gold as he pressed both hands to my head.

Unlike in my dream, he dripped water and tears on my face, stinging my eyes. The blood didn't help either. Oozing from under Sean's hand, it crawled like mosquitoes on my skin. I felt pretty.

"Calm down," McGillicuddy said. "Calm down. For God's sake, would you calm down?"

"I'm fine," I said between heaving coughs. "At least I can move my toes, so I won't have to ride the short bus."

"I meant Adam."

I stared past the pain in my head, upward at Adam's chin. Adam held me, not Sean. I hadn't recognized him upside down, without the skull and crossbones.

"Sean," Cameron called. "We've got her. Let's go."

The engine started, and the boat lurched

into high speed. Down in Adam's lap, below the sides of the boat, the motor sounded muffled, more a buzz than a roar. Without Nickelback blaring, for once.

"Let me see," McGillicuddy said, bending next to Adam.

I cringed and closed my eyes and tried to go to a different place, away from the pain, as they fumbled on my forehead. Poked at my forehead. I came back from that different place and said, "DON'T TOUCH IT."

"It's going to need stitches," McGillicuddy said. "They might have to shave your hair a little. But if they do, I'll shave mine too. So will Adam. Right, Adam?"

"It's a wonder you weren't killed," Adam cried. "It's a wonder you didn't at least put your eye out."

McGillicuddy said, "Adam, would you calm down?"

I squeezed my eyes more tightly shut.

"I can't believe you actually did it," Adam said. "I can't believe you're that stupid."

"I didn't," I mouthed. That's all I could do. Sean and Adam had been my whole life for the last couple of weeks, but it was surprising how little I cared about them when I suddenly had a throbbing headache the size of the lake. Even if I'd wanted to, I didn't have the strength to fight. Adam wouldn't have believed me, anyway.

At first, all five Vaders plus McGillicuddy crowded into the emergency room with me. The nurses kicked everyone out except Mrs. Vader. They must have mistaken her for someone motherly and soothing. She barked at people and insisted on seeing their credentials before she'd let them touch me. Then Cameron came back and said Adam had taken a swing at Sean and gotten them all kicked out of the waiting room. So Mrs. Vader herded them all home where they could beat the hell out of each other in peace. She sent McGillicuddy in to sit with me.

I didn't have a concussion, and they didn't shave my head or anything traumatic like that. After the first prick of anesthetic, my head didn't even hurt much. Which was a good thing, because McGillicuddy went to buy himself some Pop-Tarts out of the snack machine. I lay there by myself on the hospital bed and stared at the water-stained ceiling while the doc stitched me up, scolded me, and left to find me some pain pills for when the anesthetic wore off. I felt very sorry for myself and very alone until Dad showed up, with Frances.

Dad grasped my hand in both of his. "Lori. Oh, my Lori." He started to cry softly.

"Dad, I'm okay." I patted his arm: there there.

"Trevor," said Frances. Her hand was on Dad's back. "Deep breaths."

Dad sniffed a deep breath through his nose while Frances held his gaze and moved her hands in circles in the air in front of her, encouraging him to breathe therapeutically. The way they were acting, people at the hospital who didn't know them might mistake them for a couple. A very odd couple, with Frances in her tie-dyed hippie costume and Dad in his lawyer costume from the office.

"Here," I said, easing off the bed. "Lie down, Dad."

He switched places with me, never loosening his grip on my hand. "I don't want you to be scared because of this."

"She won't," Frances said.

"I won't," I said.

"I want you out there wakeboarding again tomorrow," he sobbed.

"I can't, Dad. The doc said I'm not supposed to go swimming until my stitches come out in a few days."

"Then I want you wakeboarding the day they come out. And do exactly what you were doing when you got hurt."

I thought about this. "It would be difficult to replicate."

"Do you understand me?" he said, still crying.

"Shhh," Frances said, patting his shoulder.

"Yeah, Dad," I said, looking toward McGillicuddy in the doorway. He munched his Pop-Tart. I twirled my finger beside my ear: *crazy*. McGillicuddy nodded. At least I wasn't the *only* sane person around here.

A nurse brought me some pills, which I took gladly because I didn't want my brain to hurt like that again, ever. They weren't supposed to be strong enough to put me to sleep, but they did. Or it was the medicine combined with the adrenaline draining away. The fatigue from nearly drowning, touching bryozoa, being sobbed over by a couple of he-men, etc. I'd had such a busy day.

All I knew for sure was that I stretched out on the backseat of Dad's car and slept on the way home. When we got there, I wasn't moving. They prodded me, but I could *not* see myself climbing the stairs to my room. I did *not* see why they couldn't let me sleep in the car parked in the garage. The backseat felt delicious.

McGillicuddy carried me up the stairs, and Dad tucked me into bed. Ahhhhhhh, bed had never been such a relief. Dad and McGillicuddy spoke softly in the doorway.

Dad: "She didn't even wake up. You be sure and come get her if there's a fire."

McGillicuddy: "A fire. Right, Dad."

I laughed myself back to sleep. A fire. Really! In the last twenty-four hours, I'd been through everything bad I could imagine. What else could possibly happen?

Seventeen

"Lori, when we're old enough, I want you to be my girlfriend." Sean kissed me. With his mouth still on my mouth, he pulled me off the bow seat and down into the floorboard of the boat, out of the wind.

I broke the kiss to say, "I guess this means we're old enou—"

He cut me off by kissing me. His tongue circled deep inside my mouth, and I opened for more. When I got bored with this (the idea of getting bored with making out still caused me to laugh, ho ho), I lifted my chin so he could kiss my neck. Then I turned my head so he could kiss my ear. Wow, this was the best dream ever, and so *long*! Suddenly anxious, I peered into the back of the boat to see whether the other boys were watching us. The boat was empty.

"Who's driving?" I gasped.

"You are," Sean said.

"Oh." This made me a little nervous, but not nervous enough to wake up or anything. I turned my head so he could kiss my other ear.

"Listen," he breathed. "What's that?"

"The boat motor," I murmured without thinking. "And Nickelback."

He propped himself up on his forearms and cocked his head to hear better. "Actually, I think it's JoJo." The skull and crossbones dangled above my eyes.

"Adam!" I cried, sitting bolt upright in my bed. I peered over at the clock blaring "Too Little, Too Late." No wonder the dream had lasted so long! My alarm had gone off, but I'd slept right through fifteen minutes of radio. The photo of my mother lay flat on the bedside table. McGillicuddy must have knocked it over by accident last night when he put me in bed.

"Stupid subconscious!" I slapped myself in the back of the head. "Ow!" The shock of the slap rippled through my brain and into the gash on my forehead. I cupped my hand over the stitches.

A soft knock sounded at the door. McGillicuddy leaned in without waiting for an answer. He glanced at the clock, then at me. "Breakfast is being served to the psych ward in the dining hall. You want me to send up an orderly to help you get out of bed?"

I stuck out my tongue at him. I didn't mind psych ward jokes from McGillicuddy. He was the only one who understood. Except—

"Adam came to see you."

I took in a sharp breath. "When?"

"Last night, and again this morning."

"Why didn't you wake me up?" I wailed.

"Because any other time in the history of your life, you would have snuck in my room and rearranged my sock drawer in revenge for waking you up. You know I need the argyles in the front."

"Well, what'd he say?"

McGillicuddy gathered a year's worth of wakeboarding mags and his copy of *The Right Stuff* and stacked them neatly on the floor so he could sit on the edge of my bed. "Last night he was just checking on you.

This morning he came over to say he's taking the day off work. But he wanted you to know, he's through."

"He's through? With what?" With Sean? Fighting with Sean?

"With you."

Of course he was through with me. He'd told me as much while I bled in his lap yesterday. As long as I heard it with my own ears, I could hope I'd misread the whole situation. Hearing it from McGillicuddy made it real. Almost. "Are you making this up?"

"No. He's really mad at you. I've never seen him this mad. Not even at Sean." McGillicuddy thumbed through *The Right Stuff* to make sure I hadn't gotten marshmallow on it. "But I want you to know some good will come out of your crash. It's inspired me to do something I've wanted to do for a long time."

"Remove your own appendix?"

"Ask Tammy out."

My head hurt. "Tammy? Why?"

"I think she's been coming to the Vaders' parties to see me. I know, I know, this seems as impossible to me as it does to you, but I really think she likes me."

I grunted a little with the increasing

pain in my head. I didn't want to tell him this, but it might save him some humiliation later. "McGillicuddy, you're wrong. She's been coming to the Vaders' parties to see *me*. We're friends."

He squinted at me. "Why do you think so?"

"She told me so."

"Couldn't it be one of those schemes, like you and Adam are pulling on Sean? She's pretending to be your friend so she can see me without admitting that's why she's at the party."

"Tammy wouldn't do that to me," I said. My pulse began to race, and my head throbbed harder with every heartbeat. "What do you mean, one of those schemes like Adam and I are pulling on Sean?"

"I figure if you can brain yourself on a pontoon boat just to get a boy to ask you out, I can ask a girl out and brave a little rejection."

Now I winced against the throbbing in my head. "Adam told you I crashed just to get Sean to ask me out?"

"Yeah. He told me you've faked going out from the beginning. He's *really mad* about you crashing." McGillicuddy leaned across the bed and nabbed his copy of *The Hunt for Red October*, which I'd been telling him since last summer I did *not* borrow, when in actuality I had lost it under some (clean!) laundry and didn't come across it until last week. "Adam and Sean have always fought," McGillicuddy said, tucking the book under his arm for safekeeping. "But you've made it a million times worse. Can you imagine the five of us wakeboarding together for the rest of the summer?"

"No," I admitted. It sounded about as fun as getting a tooth pulled every afternoon. "But I didn't start this in the first place. Sean did. Sean stole Rachel from Adam."

"Adam never liked Rachel anyway," McGillicuddy said. "He was madder about the insult than the girl. He was in love with you. If it hadn't been for you wanting to fool Sean, Adam would have simmered down eventually and let Sean have Rachel. We'd be back to normal by now."

"Reverse, please," I said. "Adam was in love with—"

"You. Where did I go wrong? I raised a little brother, not a femme fatale."

I didn't quite get it. Could Adam have

been telling me the truth about his plot? It seemed too good to be true, and too awful if I had screwed this up. "Did Adam *say* he's in love with me?"

"*Was* in love with you. Yes, that's what he said. How the hell else would I know? I wish I didn't. This place is getting to be like that awful girls' show, what's it called? The chicks in my dorm call dibs on the TV in the rec center and won't let us watch basketball."

"*Laguna Beach*?"

"Yes!"

"Get out of my room."

As he stood, I made a weak grab for *The Hunt for Red October*, but he dodged me. He closed the door behind him.

Adam was in love with me. He wasn't just saying it to keep me with him while he made Sean jealous. He was in love with me.

Head throbbing, I looked around my room, which still reflected the boy I'd been before I started transforming myself. I hadn't gotten around to a room makeover with purple flowers and a fuzzy pink ottoman. As the air conditioning clicked on, the fighter jet models I'd built from kits swayed at the end of their strings near the ceiling. I was a little brother. I was a mess.

Adam had been in love with me, just like this.

And now he wasn't.

It was a good thing Advil took care of my headache. If I'd had to stay out of work and spend the day at home, I would have driven myself insane (if I wasn't already). As it was, I showered faster than usual to make up for lost time, taking care to keep my stitches out of the spray. I ate breakfast as usual, except Dad gave me a big hug and sobbed a little into my hair. As usual, McGillicuddy and I opened the door to hike across our yard and the Vaders' to the marina—

—and there stood Sean with his finger on the doorbell. He asked me brightly, "Will you go to the party tonight with me?"

My brain said, *Hooray! I'm going out with Sean! My time has come!*

My body was strangely quiet. There was no happy skin. My brain reached down through my nerve endings to poke at my heart and make sure it was okay. My heart said, *Eh*. At this point I realized I *did* need to go back to the shrink. I sagged against the doorjamb, rolled my eyes, and uttered something very unladylike.

McGillicuddy stepped around me and wagged his cell phone between his fingers. With a pointed look at Sean, he told me, "Call me if you need me."

"I could take you," Sean shouted after McGillicuddy. "Bring it on." His voice echoed around the garage. Then he turned back to me and sighed, "I was afraid you'd say that. Look, I told my dad we'd come to work a little late this morning because we're going to fish your wakeboard out of the lake. Let's talk."

I followed him down to my pier, where he'd tied the wakeboarding boat. Clearly it *did* occur to him to dock in a certain place to save *someone* a long walk. Himself. Just not me. We stepped in, and I looked around on the floor. "Who cleaned the blood out of the boat for me? I was going to do it this morning."

"Adam," Sean said. "When we get to the pontoon boat, you've got to tell me this story. He was saying it was his fault and crying the whole time. Pussy." He slapped his hand over his mouth. "Sorry. I almost forgot you weren't a guy." Before I could offer a choice response, he cranked the motor and the Nickelback.

As we zoomed toward the pontoon boat, I noticed that a dump truck had mistakenly unloaded a pile of soot onto the side of the bridge. The closer we got, the more clearly I could see it wasn't a pile of soot after all but carefully applied spray paint marking out the letters AOAN LOVES LOKI. Adam had been busy. He must have gone out in the motorboat in the near-dark last night, or the near-dark this morning. He wanted to get the offensive words off the bridge as quickly as he could. They would have haunted him until he got rid of them. He hated me that much.

"Junior!" Sean stood in front of me, clapping his hands. "McGillicuddy Part Deux!" He'd stopped the boat next to the pontoon boat. "McGillicuddy left your wakeboard floating here, so let's check under the pontoon boat first." He handed me one of the oars that motorboats carry in case their engines stop when they run over logs. As we poked around under the pontoons, he asked, "Why's Adam so pissed at you?"

"It's complicated. We've only been going out to make you and Rachel mad." I couldn't believe I was telling him this. But my brilliant ploys had gotten me into this fix, and I'd lost hope they could get me out. Also, I must have bled out my last lick of sense. "I've sort of had a thing for you."

He pulled his oar from under the boat and put all his weight on it, like he needed it to keep him from collapsing. "*You*? Have a thing for *me*?"

"*Had*."

He made a face. "Ugh!"

This should have been the low point of my life, the one I'd dreaded for over a decade: rejection by Sean. Now that it had finally happened, I didn't feel humiliated. I was angry. "What do you mean, *ugh*? You flirted with me a couple of weeks ago, before your first party. Remember wiping bryozoa on me? That's the mating dance of the brain-dead Vader brothers."

"Oh, yeah! I'd forgotten all about the bryozoa." He waved his hand in the air, dismissing the bryozoa incident like a pesky yellow jacket. "Adam was acting protective of you that day for some reason. I got the idea he might like you a little. So I figured I'd push his buttons. I can't see myself really coming on to you, ever." He shoved his oar under the boat again. "No offense."

"None taken, you ass."

He glanced sideways at me. "When I said 'Ugh,' I just meant, 'Ugh, what could Buddy possibly see in little old me?'"

Sure you did. "I honestly can't remember," I said, poking my oar under the boat, too. "Anyway, Adam thinks I crashed into the pontoon boat on purpose so you could close the wakeboarding show again, and you'd like me better. I didn't, but Adam thinks I did." I ran my finger over the little dent my thick skull had made in the aluminum side of the boat. "I guess he was willing to take the fake love just so far."

"So you've faked hooking up."

I glanced toward the bridge, at the scribble that once had said AOAN LOVES LOKI. "Yeah."

"You faked flirting with each other on the desk in the living room."

"Yeah." It hadn't *felt* like faking, but what did I know?

"You faked making out on the end of the dock at the party last Friday? And disappearing into the lake? Because that was convincing."

"Yes. I mean, we really made out, but we weren't really in love." At least, I hadn't realized it at the time.

"That little shit!" he yelled so loudly that I worried about the innocent ears of Frances and the Harbarger children around the bend. I imagined Frances pretending she hadn't heard a thing as the shout echoed around their fenced yard.

"Now why are *you* so pissed?" I asked.

"Because it worked! He stole Rachel from me!"

I stomped my foot on the floor of the boat, like a girl. "You stole Rachel from him in the first place, just to make him mad. Even if you *thought* you really liked her by the time she broke up with you, she only seemed like something you'd want because Adam had her in the first place."

He brought in his oar again and leaned on it. "I may be shallow, Lori, but I'm not a monster." He gazed downstream. "I don't think your wakeboard's under here. Maybe the current caught it."

I looked downstream, too, in the general direction of the dam several miles away. My wakeboard had probably gotten stuck in one of the gates and cut off the power supply to the tri-county area. The way my morning was going, the hydroelectric police would be waiting for me on the marina dock.

"Let's try one more place." He cranked the engine, drove to the nearby bank, and cut the power again. As the boat drifted, we used the oars to shift the logs and leaves washed up against the edge of the woods. "You think I'm a monster," he said quietly.

"I think we all are."

A gust of wind blew us along faster. It swooped through the woods, swaying the trees and littering us with blossoms and leaves and delicate tree crap.

"Well," he finally said. "I didn't steal Rachel just to make Adam mad. I *pretended* that's what I was doing. That's what Adam would think anyway. But really, I've been into her for so long. I couldn't stand the thought of going to college without finding out if she liked me, too."

I was going to yell at him for being so selfish until it occurred to me that this was pretty much how I'd felt about *him*.

"I've seen the way she looks at Adam," he went on. "Girls don't look at me like that. They look at me, sure, but not like that."

Cunning as Sean was about other people,

surely he couldn't be this obtuse about himself? In exasperation, I pointed out, "You don't look at *them* like that."

"I look at Rachel like that. And she says she can tell from the way I treat Adam that I have no soul. I could have sworn I did." He laughed.

Rachel might have more sense than I'd given her credit for. She'd never actually insulted me, besides calling me a 'ho to her friends when I did the secret handshake with Adam, which was understandable. I had no reason to dislike her, other than the obvious boy-ploys. And no reason at all to think she was stupid.

"But over the last couple of weeks," Sean continued, "I've seen how good you and Adam are together. And how good Rachel and I are together. Maybe Adam and Rachel are good together, too, but if they are, I'd like to rip Rachel's heart out and throw it down in the driveway and drive back and forth over it in my truck a couple of times and give it back to her. I know you feel the same way about Adam."

I stared at him and wondered what my mother had been thinking.

"I don't think we need to worry about

that, though," he said. "Rachel wants to get back with Adam, but Adam doesn't want Rachel, if you can believe that! He called her last night after he dried up and had this, like, *reasonable, adult* conversation with her. He told her it was over between them, and not just because she'd made out with me when I snapped my fingers. He went out with her in the first place to make you jealous."

None of this sounded like something Adam would share with Sean on purpose. McGillicuddy, maybe, or Cameron, but not Sean. "Did you listen in on this conversation?"

Sean gave me this *how dare you insinuate such a thing* look. Which told me, yes, he had listened in on this conversation.

He went on, "So we know they won't get back together. If they do look like they're getting back together at the party tonight, Adam will be faking. All we have to do to get him back with you is convince him you're better than nothing. Which . . ." He looked me up and down, then shrugged.

The wind gusted again, lifting sections of his light brown hair, and flattening his T-shirt against his strong chest. He was a lot like Adam, and completely different. I said, "You are a sad, sad little man."

"I am what I am. So, I know this will sound kind of gross, but will you make out with me at the party?"

I poked at the shoreline with my oar. "This is a bad idea. It was a bad idea the first time I had it, and it's a bad idea now." But I might as well try something to get Adam back, right? I'd hit bottom. Nothing we did could make things worse.

"If you won't do it for yourself, do it for me. Lori, I'm in love with Rachel. That's never happened to me before. I'm not willing to let that go without a fight. And if you feel the same way about Adam, seems like you wouldn't let it go, either." He took a few steps closer to me in the boat. "He holds a grudge, you know."

I snorted. "I know." Nothing had ever been more obvious.

"You can't just hope he'll come around someday. He won't. You have to bring him back. Hey, what do we have here?" He leaned way over the side of the boat, grabbed a flower-printed edge underneath a log, and brought up my dripping wakeboard. Handing it to me, he said, "Your chariot, mademoiselle."

It was exactly like something Adam

would say. I clung to the wet wakeboard and squeezed my eyes shut to keep from crying. "Okay," I said. "I'll do it. Okay."

It all would have been hilarious if it hadn't sucked.

Eighteen

And I couldn't go through with it. When McGillicuddy said he was heading for the party, I stayed behind. I actually started the enormous project of picking up all the books and magazines scattered three deep on the floor of my room. After about an hour and hardly any progress, I realized that by shelving them, I was messing up a filing system I didn't even know I had. Books I wanted to read again were thrown on one side of my bed. Bad books were abandoned by the window. Wakeboarding mags were strewn from my dresser to my desk in approximate order of how hot the boys were in them, and so forth. I gave up and sat downstairs in the den with my dad for a long time, watching *Dirty Jobs*.

My cell phone rang. I pried it from the pocket of my tight miniskirt. I knew girls were supposed to carry purses instead of stuffing everything in their pockets, but I needed to ease into this transition over the coming year. Sirens weren't built in a day. "Hello?"

Sean was on the other end of the line, making chicken noises.

I hung up and said bye to my dad. Again, I didn't notify him what was going on with my many suitors. I figured the situation would change anyway in the next fifteen minutes or so.

Sean stood in the doorway of the Vaders' house, letting all the air conditioning out into the hot night. Waiting for me. "Where have you been?"

"Duh, I've been next d—"

He grabbed me, pulled me into the foyer, and slammed the door. "Rachel and Adam are inside talking. *To each other!* And I've told everybody here that you and I are together. When you didn't show up, it looked like you didn't love me as much as I love you."

"Stop the presses."

"So we need to make up for lost time."

He body-slammed me against the wall and stuck his tongue in my mouth.

Well, I just let him do it. Why not? I let him slide his hands up and down my sides, too, in case that helped the cause. If he wanted to touch my boobs, I would need to take that under advisement, but otherwise I found I had a very high tolerance for a handsome ass of a boy using me as target practice.

Besides, out the corner of my eye, I could see Holly and Beige watch us from the end of the hall. They disappeared around the corner. Next a couple of guys from my algebra class walked very slowly by the opening, pretending not to watch us.

Sean came up for breath. I tried not to gasp quite as hard as I had after bashing my head and nearly drowning.

"How many gawkers is that?" he asked.

"Four," I said. "Is that enough to spread it around the party? And how can you stand to kiss a girl like that when you don't feel anything for her?"

He rubbed the back of my neck, like a lover. "I feel *something* for you. You clean up okay. Don't you feel *something* for me?"

I shook my head. "I'm not feeling you, dog."

"Don't shake your head," he said through his teeth. "We're going into the party now. Don't do anything negative. Agree with everything I say. Laugh a lot. Can you put your hands on my crotch?"

"Why, hell no, I cannot." I didn't remember anything like this happening in *Pride and Prejudice*. "Can I find Tammy, take her to the bathroom with me, and giggle about you?"

His eyes widened in admiration. "That would be awesome!"

I was getting good at this. I gave him a peck on his stylishly stubbly cheek, patted his ass, and walked into the living room.

Every head snapped up to watch me.

Including Adam's. There were thirty-something people in the shadowy room, and I saw him right away. He sat on the couch with Rachel, exactly where Sean had sat with her the night he insulted me. Adam wasn't wrapped around Rachel like Sean had been. He wasn't touching her at all. He was talking to her. They could have been friends.

So they weren't doing anything to make me jealous. All he did was look up at me with such fury in those blue eyes that I knew I was going to throw up.

"Help," I croaked, putting a hand on Tammy's shoulder.

She looked around at me. She looked at the boys she'd been talking with: Cameron and McGillicuddy. "Can Cameron help you?" she asked me coldly. "They're his brothers, so he could help you better. *Bill* and I were talking."

Hadn't she heard Sean's blitzkrieg rumors? I wasn't pretending to hook up with Adam to get Sean. Surprise! I was pretending to hook up with Sean to get Adam, and if ever something was giggle-in-the-bathroom material, this was it. I was calculating how much of this to divulge to her while Cameron and McGillicuddy were listening, when something else clicked in my brain. "Are y'all going out?"

"Yes!" McGillicuddy beamed.

Tammy beamed too, then tried to hold the smile as she realized she'd been busted.

"So," I said to Tammy, "when you told me you came to the last party to see me, really you were using that as an excuse to see McGillicuddy."

"I didn't mean to hurt your feelings," Tammy said distantly, a tone she'd never used with me before. The tone Beige used all the time. "I guess I didn't understand you and I were that close."

"I guess it was my mistake," I said.

"I want to go back to college," Cameron said. "Linear Differential Equations class will seem so relaxing after this summer."

McGillicuddy frowned at Tammy, then moved toward me like he would pull me aside and talk to me. But McGillicuddy didn't go out much. He'd actually asked someone out! I didn't want to mess up this thing with Tammy for him. Not over some weird girl-jealousy that I didn't even understand completely.

"I gotta do something," I mumbled, pulling the skull and crossbones from my pocket. This took a couple of tries when my fist got stuck.

Across the room, Sean stood with some of his many friends. Down by his side, where the crowd couldn't see, he motioned to me. Rachel and her friends were right behind him. If I went to him, he'd make sure they saw everything that counted.

From the sofa on the other side of the room, Adam glared at me.

I took a step toward Adam. The force of his glare was like a magnet turned the wrong way against another. I took another step toward him and felt the force in my stomach. I would never be able to reach him in the face of such force. Plus Scooter Ledbetter was trying to start a mosh pit in the center of the room. So I skirted the force like I was headed out the door to the deck. Then, when Adam bit his lip and looked down, I snuck past the repellant force and plopped next to him on the couch.

"Here." I held out the skull and cross-bones in my sweaty palm. Attractive! It didn't matter any more. "Look," I said in a rush, "I didn't crash into the pontoon boat to get Sean. Even I am not that unbalanced."

His mouth moved so little that I almost thought he used telepathy to tell me, "I don't believe you."

"No shit. And I'm sorry about the PDA with Sean. I don't know what I was thinking, Adam. I want another chance with you, and I *know* that wasn't the way to get it."

"That's okay," he said so brightly, so unlike him, that I knew something evil was coming. "I like Sean taking my seconds."

"See, that's the problem," I snapped, angry again despite myself. "You say you love me, but you're always looking over your shoulder for Sean."

"And you're always looking over *your* shoulder for Sean. Or Holly, or Beige." The Foo Fighters song booming through the room ended at the precise moment he said, "Or whoever's made you change from what you were into a first-class bitch."

Only a moment more of silence ticked by before Fall Out Boy started. But the damage was done. People at the edge of the crowd were slow to start dancing again. They thought we couldn't hear them over the music as they yelled in clear voices, "Did you hear what Adam called Lori?"

I told myself he wouldn't have said anything so horrible to me if he weren't jealous. Of course, I'd told myself the same thing when Sean mentioned the shrink. But Sean was Sean, and Adam was Adam. And while I was trying to use my intimidating brain power to turn myself into water vapor and vanish into thin air, Adam snatched the skull and crossbones from my open palm. "I have just the use for this," he said as he stomped out the door to the deck.

I left my sparkly shoes on the floor next to the couch. I knew that jig was up. But even in my bare feet, I didn't make it outside before Adam was on the ground far below, halfway to the dock. Possibly he'd jumped over the deck railing.

I dashed down the stairs. Sean called to me from the deck above me. I dashed faster. This was no time to save face. I had a terrible feeling about that skull and crossbones.

Sure enough, by the time I'd pushed through the crowd in the yard and the wall of people on the dock, Adam was sitting with the boys playing quarters. I stepped forward to stop him. It was too late. Instead of a quarter, he bounced the pendant on the dock. And instead of ringing the cup, the skull and crossbones slipped between two planks, into the lake.

"Ohhhhhh!" said the other boys.

"Get it," I told Adam.

He said thoughtfully, "No."

I pictured it sinking through the water, but it wasn't heavy enough to stay in one place on the bottom. The current would sweep it away if he didn't hurry. "I bought it for you!" I shrieked.

"I wore it for you," he said evenly. "And now I'm through with it."

I shoved back through the wall of people,

jumped into Mr. Vader's personal fishing boat tied on one side of the dock, and grabbed a big waterproof flashlight. I didn't have to push through the wall of people on my way back because they saw me coming and got out of my way. I walked straight through the game of quarters, scattering frightened boys. I sensed rather than saw Adam's hand reach for my ankle and miss as I hopped into the lake in my adorable clothes.

The water was warm and black. Oops. I clicked the button on the flashlight and directed the beam underneath the pier. The water was only about eight feet deep here, so I was able to kick down to the rocky bottom, where I thought the pendant had fallen through.

In the eerie green light, I saw it glinting on a big branch the boys had lodged under the dock to attract fish. That was bad enough, because wood got slimy in water. But this was worse: the pendant glinted from its resting place in A GLOB OF BRYOZOA clinging to the branch. Ugh, ugh, ugh, and the pendant moved as the bryozoa bobbed in the current. Any second now, the skull and crossbones would tumble deep into the lake, lost forever.

My breath was gone. I swam toward the

surface to collect one more breath. I didn't expect half the school to be peering over the side of the dock, watching for me in the darkness. That was okay. I was on a mission to PLUNGE MY HAND INTO THE BRYOZOA OH MY GOD. I took my breath and dove back down—

And someone on the dock grabbed me around the waist. Someone strong who wasn't dislodged from the dock when I struggled. Adam lifted me backward out of the water.

"Let me go!" I hollered, not looking at him, still leaning toward the water and trying to struggle free. The flashlight clattered to the dock. "I saw it. I can still get it. Let me go!"

"You're not supposed to get your stitches wet," he said.

I wanted to point out that he would not know this, since he didn't stick around the emergency room long enough to hear what the doctor had to say. Then I remembered Adam had a lot more experience with stitches than I did.

And then, out the corner of my eye, I saw a blur, and Adam was gone. An enormous splash backed everyone away from the water. Adam and Sean flailed in the lake.

"Get their parents," I said over my shoulder. If Cameron or McGillicuddy had been there, they would have stepped forward before now. And Sean's friends and Adam's friends never intervened, like fights between brothers were somehow sacred. I watched Adam and Sean in the water to make sure neither of them went down for too long—though there wasn't much I could have done if they had. Nothing seemed to be happening behind me. The crowd watched the show as attentively as I did. I turned around and screamed, "Go get their parents!" Three people ran up the dock and through the yard.

I jumped out of the way as one of the boys hauled himself up the ladder. He snapped his legs up before the other boy could drag him back into the lake. But then the second boy grabbed the top of the ladder, swung himself onto the dock, and tackled the first.

There didn't seem much point in explaining to Adam that Sean had only attacked him because Sean and I were pretending to be a couple and trying to make Adam jealous. After one of them had hit the other, it didn't really matter why anymore, at least not to them. I bent as close to them as I dared and hollered, "I've already told your parents."

"Sean, stop," came Rachel's voice from the crowd, ever-helpful.

I expected them to roll toward me. I'd have to jump out of the way as they wrestled on the dock and caught each other in various choke holds. Instead, the boy on top punched the one on bottom, a pop to the nose. The fight came to an abrupt stop.

The crowd gasped. They murmured, "No, that's Adam on top. *Adam* kicked *Sean's* ass."

Adam sat on Sean's chest, his right fist clenching and unclenching. I couldn't see his face or Sean's in the dim light, but I could tell from the way they held themselves that they were giving each other the evil eye. And I knew I shouldn't be worried anymore about pulling Sean off Adam, protecting Adam from Sean.

Adam said so quietly I could hardly hear him over the waves lapping against the dock, "Don't you ever hit me again."

The murmur up the hill increased, and the crowd in the yard began to part. Mr.

Vader was coming. But it was Mrs. Vader who came running in her bathrobe.

"Sean!" she called when she hadn't even hit the dock yet. "Sean, get *off* him!" As the crowd slowed her down, she said, "You two have *got* to stop doing this. You're going to kill each other." She made it through the wall of people and stopped short.

"I'm through," Adam said. He eased off Sean and stood up.

Sean sat up, looking down. His nose streamed blood.

Mr. Vader said behind us, "Hey. Is that my beer?"

I'd seen enough. I pushed my way through the crowd, up the pier, into the grass. Knots of people followed me with their eyes, turning as I passed. Cameron, McGillicuddy, and Tammy jogged down from the house. Tammy called to me. I shook my head and kept going. They didn't come toward me. They must have seen the expression on my face.

When I reached the darkest shadows of the trees between our houses, I looked back. Mrs. Vader stood in front of Adam in their yard, with her hands on her hips. He shivered in his soaked clothes. She put out her arms for him. He walked into her embrace and put his head down on her shoulder. She rubbed his back to warm him.

Furious as I was with him, I hoped he didn't get in too much trouble—about the beer, and especially about the fight with Sean. I hoped his parents understood this fight was inevitable, with or without Rachel and me and *Laguna Beach*. And that tonight was the first night of the rest of his life.

Nineteen

It was not, however, the first night of the rest of *my* life. It was night 5,843, and felt like it.

I stepped into the kitchen and closed the door. I dripped all over the floor. Dad freaked out about stuff like this. Someone might slip! I'd have to find a towel in the laundry room and drag it behind me all the way to the den—unless, of course, he heard me come in and called to me to ask me how my night went. Then I'd have an excuse to skip the towel. I could sit in his lap, even though I was soaked. I could break down, and he could tell me what to do about Adam.

He didn't call to me. Maybe he hadn't heard me in my bare feet. I opened and closed some kitchen drawers gratuitously. Still he didn't call to me.

I gave up, got a towel out of the laundry room, and scooted it across the floor with my feet, catching the water that dripped from me. As I headed through the den to the stairs up to my room, I saw Dad. He'd fallen asleep on the sofa in front of the TV, cell phone gripped on his chest. I was on my own.

I walked up the stairs, which took more energy than usual. There were a lot of stairs. Thirteen, to be exact:

1. Made
2. You
3. Change
4. From
5. What
6. You
7. Were
8. In
9. To
10. A
11. First
12. Class
13. Bitch

By the time I got to the top, I was pooped, and not furious anymore. Confused and hurt about Tammy. Hurt and sad about Adam.

A long time passed before I realized I was standing in my dark room, listening to the laughter and music from the party outside.

Closing my door behind me, I slid my wet clothes off. Oh God, dead wet cell phone in my skirt pocket. There went my birthday money from my grandparents. I didn't need to turn on the light to find my mother's sweet sixteen disco dress in my closet, because it practically glowed in the dark. I slipped it on and walked to the window.

Sean and Adam lay on that strip of grass between our yards where they liked to fight each other because their mom couldn't see them from their house. Adam and Sean had finally killed each other! No—Adam's arms were behind his head. Sean's legs were bent, with one foot propped casually on the opposite knee. They watched the stars, talking.

Talking!

Adam sat up. He wore his sweatshirt with his football number on the back, the one I'd borrowed last weekend. He shook a little like he was shivering again. He stuck his hands in his pockets. He pulled out one hand and looked at it, then looked over his shoulder at my house. He'd found my eyelash comb.

Maybe he saw my dress glowing in the moonlight, because he turned all the way around to stare. Now Sean sat up and turned around, too. Or maybe it was Sean and then Adam. I couldn't tell them apart in the dark. It didn't matter now, anyway. Bwa-ha-ha, I hope I creeped them out like Miss Havisham (*Great Expectations*, eighth grade English).

But *one* of them was Adam. Tingles crept up my arms and across my chest at the thought of him watching me. This would have to stop. Pining after Sean had been bad enough. At least I'd always thought pining after Sean would have a happy ending. I *knew* no good would come from pining after Adam. Plus it was a lot more real to me now, not a cartoon relationship lost but a real boyfriend, a real friend. I choked back a sob as my throat closed up.

I watched him for a little longer. Yes, I could tell him from Sean, even at a distance, even in the dark. The way he moved his head, the way he tapped his fingers on the ground in that fidget I'd fallen in love with. That could have been me instead of Sean, sitting with Adam in the dark. But there wasn't a way to fix this.

Ten years from now, I'd be married to someone I'd met at college. Adam would be married to someone he'd met on the bomb squad. We'd all come home to visit our parents at Thanksgiving. Adam and I would see each other out on the docks. We would feel obliged to talk for a few minutes and laugh uncomfortably about this one summer that had ruined our friendship forever. And then we'd walk away.

I looked at the clock on my bedside table behind me. 12:02. I closed the window shade, blocking out the party and Sean and Adam. I slipped off the disco dress and folded it into a big box with the scrapbook Mom and I had made to fill in with pictures of my sixteenth birthday. Standing in a chair precariously balanced on books, mags, and Mr. Wuggles—God only knew what was under there, really—I slid the box onto a shelf in the top of my closet. Where it belonged.

I woke to Kelly Clarkson's "Breakaway."

My body had gotten used to waking at this time. I didn't remember my dreams.

I would miss them.

But I tried to shake it off. I tried not to wish Adam would show up with a birthday present for me—even though I'd forgotten to get one for *him*! I would have the usual birthday breakfast with Dad and McGillicuddy, just like every year, and then I'd try to get through my first-ever day of avoiding my ex-best friend. While I worked at his parents' marina. And he worked there too. Easy.

For breakfast, Dad made me pancakes with blueberries in the shape of smiley faces, because he was a dork. Between the butter and the syrup, McGillicuddy handed me a long tube-shaped present. Actually it was just a wrapping paper tube with the wrapping paper still on it, and something rolled up inside. Boys were like that. He saw my look and shrugged. "It would have been a waste of perfectly good wrapping paper. This worked."

Still giving him the look, I pulled out the contents of the tube and unrolled a wakeboarding poster. "Dallas Friday!" I exclaimed. "Dallas Friday shattered her femur doing a whirlybird."

"I thought it was perfect for the occasion," McGillicuddy said. "Fearless."

Dad cleared his throat and pushed a little box across the table to me. It was beautifully wrapped with an intricate bow that most girls would keep on their bulletin boards. Obviously wrapped in a store. I slipped the bow off intact and tried to unstick the paper without tearing it. It tore by accident and then, what the hell, I ripped it off.

I flipped open the velvet ring box. Inside was a silver ring with pearls and diamonds. It looked real. Was I supposed to bite it to make sure? No, that was gold coins in cowboy movies. It also looked vaguely familiar. "You didn't get this at the store."

"I had them check the settings," Dad said. "They cleaned it and wrapped it for you."

I examined the ring more closely. "It belonged to Mom."

"Her parents gave it to her for her sixteenth birthday."

I looked into his eyes, so full of concern. We had a touching moment. Then of course McGillicuddy dropped his fork and went under the table to hunt for it, and it was hard to keep the touching moment going while McGillicuddy sat on my toes. "Ow!" I kicked him.

"When you were younger," Dad said, "I thought you'd never wear it, because it wasn't your style. Lately, I'm not so sure. I thought I should give you the choice."

I freed it from the box and slipped it onto my finger. It was a crazy ring, diamonds glinting in contrast with the smooth pearls. And it was heavy. If I ever got in a fix in a dark alley, I could use it as brass knuckles. Or if I was cornered on a rooftop, I could hook it onto a clothesline and slide to freedom like James Bond. Don't try this at home.

"I'll wear it because it's a part of me," I said. "Thank you, Dad." I walked around the table and hugged him. Then I sat back down, took another bite of pancake, and stared straight ahead at the empty chair.

And I realized for the first time ever that we kept an empty chair at the table. There were three of us. You would think we would have three chairs normally, and bring in a fourth when Adam came to dinner, which clearly wouldn't be happening anymore. It wasn't like the table was square, and a chair missing from the fourth side would be conspicuous. The table was round, and could have three chairs as easily as four or five or eight.

I was swallowing my pancakes in order to point this out when Dad said, "I need to tell you something, Bill. I don't want you to see me on the bank during the wakeboarding show and wipe out because of the shock. We've had enough wakeboard falls for one lifetime." He took a sip of coffee. "I have a date for the Crappie Festival." He took another sip of coffee. "It's Frances."

I sat still, thinking back to that talk I'd had with Frances. She'd said, *You're the only one who comes to visit. Except—*

McGillicuddy didn't budge, either. Dad must have taken our non-reaction as disapproval. "I never said anything while she worked here," he hurried on. "I never did anything. We were coping so well, for a grieving family—"

"Except for when you sent me to the shrink," I pointed out.

He continued more loudly, "—and I was terrified of messing that up." He turned to McGillicuddy. "But now you've got a foot or two out the door." He turned to me. "And you're—" He sighed. "Grown. I thought it would be okay now." He took still another sip of coffee, nonchalant, but his eyes darted to McGillicuddy and me in turn. "Even if it's not okay, I'm still going out with her."

We sat in silence a few moments more. Then McGillicuddy hollered, "Fanny the Nanny!"

"It's all very *Jane Eyre* of you, Dad," I said. McGillicuddy had read *Jane Eyre* in ninth grade English, and then *I'd* read it in ninth grade English. We'd wished we had Frances back just so we could make *Jane Eyre* jokes.

McGillicuddy snorted. "Hide the lighter fluid."

"Check the attic," I said.

Dad sat back in his chair, relaxing a little.

"No wonder she used to get so mad when Sean sang to her from *The Sound of Music*," McGillicuddy said.

"Does this mean we have to start drinking soy milk again?" I asked Dad.

"I'm glad we've gotten this settled," Dad said. "Bill, what'd you dream about?"

McGillicuddy blinked at the change of subject. "I can't tell you."

"Why not?" I grinned.

"She's a real person."

I took this as my cue to head for the marina. Dad would probably coax the dream out of McGillicuddy—Dad was a lawyer, after all—and I didn't particularly want to hear just then about Tammy beating McGillicuddy at wrestling in chocolate pudding.

But McGillicuddy stood when I did. Dad looked up at him and said, "You take care of your sister today."

McGillicuddy shrugged. "How?"

Dad looked at me. "And you watch out for those boys."

It was way too early in the morning for a breakdown, so I squeezed my eyes shut to hold back the tears and stepped out the door, calling, "I'm afraid I have nothing to be afraid of."

Twenty

In the garage, balanced on the handle of the seed spreader, looking out of place between the lawnmower and the tiller, was a long-stemmed pink rose.

McGillicuddy passed me. I called, "Tammy left you a gag gift."

He hardly glanced at the rose on his way out the garage door. "Pink isn't my color."

Frances must have left it as a joke for Dad, then. I should take it into the kitchen before it wilted. Almost wishing it were mine, I ran my finger across a soft petal. My hand found a pink ribbon tied around the stem, then a tag hanging from the ribbon. The tag said in Adam's scrawl, "YES it's for you." I let a little laugh escape even as my eyes filled with tears.

He'd called me a bitch. I wasn't running back to him when he left me one rose. On the other hand, there was no need to stuff it down the garbage disposal. Maybe Adam and I could be friends again after all. Someday. Besides, I adored the scent of roses: perfume and dirt. I put the blossom to my nose, inhaled deeply, grinned, and headed to work.

Another rose lay atop the woodpile.

A third was tied to an oak tree with a hangman's noose fashioned from kudzu vine.

A fourth stuck out of a broken brick in the seawall.

A fifth lay across the handles of the doors into the marina. They all smelled so lovely, my blood pressure hardly went up when Mrs. Vader shrieked at me, "Where have you been?"

She must have freaked out because the marina was already swamped with customers. The Crappy Festivities today were divided among the town swimming park and the three biggest marinas on this section of the lake, including ours. We got the crowning of the Crappy Queen. I wished we got a more interesting event, such as the Crappy Toss. I could have thrown a dead fish as far up the beach as anybody. The Crappy Queen contest was just a bunch of high school girls parading up and down the wharf as Mr. Vader called their names and announced the weights of the biggest fish they'd caught all year, and what bait they'd used. At least the event did its job of bringing customers in.

Well, if Mrs. Vader wanted me there sooner, she should have told me the day before. "Where have I been?" I repeated. "I get asked that a lot for some reason."

She took the roses from me without comment and shoved me into the show-room, where a small crowd of people in shorts and flip-flops milled between the displays. "It's been a revolving door in here since we opened this morning," she hissed. "People want to buy wakeboards, and they want to buy them from *you*."

"Wow! Really?" I'd feel a little guilty selling people wakeboards, considering my experience two days before. But after all, my wreck was caused by a brain cloud and a broken heart, not equipment failure. I patted my head to make sure my bangs hung down over my stitches.

"Yes, really!" Mrs. Vader said. "Adam's been covering for you, but he just mumbles at customers."

"Where *is* Ad—," I started to ask. Then I saw his broad back, and the door to the warehouse closed behind him. Where he'd stood, a rose protruded from behind a Liquid Force on the wall.

He'd called me a bitch. I wasn't running back to him when he left me six roses. But I did extract the new rose carefully and put it with the others in the vase Mrs. Vader set on the counter. Then I found another rolled up in the boat twine, and still another lying across the containers of worms.

In the late morning, as I manned the cash register (after pulling out the rose inside), Dad and Frances came in. My heart pounded when I saw Frances. I wanted to vault over the counter and throw my arms around her. Instead, I asked her in a British accent, "Please, marm, are you to be my new mother?"

"Lori!" my dad burst out. Flushing red, he realized he desperately needed a new slalom ski *right then*, and bolted for the display.

Frances watched him go. "Very funny," she told me through her teeth. Then she leaned across the counter, kissed me on the forehead, and gave me a grudging smile. "Happy birthday."

"Thank you, marm."

She reached for my hand. "What a beautiful ring." She moved my finger back and forth so the ring glittered under the fluorescent lights, and smiled at me again. "Your mother would be proud of you."

"What a pretty dress," I said. "Is it hemp?"

Holding her chin high, she said self-righteously, "It's organic cotton." She took a long whiff of the roses. "You and Adam have gotten yourselves in a mess, I hear. 'Oh, what a tangled web we weave, when first we practice to deceive!' Sir Walter Scott."

I patted her hand. "That's nice, dear."

"'An honest man's the noblest work of God.' Alexander Pope."

I squinted across the showroom. "I think I have a customer."

My dad recovered and decided he could put off that slalom ski purchase after all. He came to the counter, put his hand on Frances's back, and asked her, "Is Lori giving you lip?"

"She's making fun of me!" Frances

exclaimed in mock astonishment. "I'm offering her aphorisms and she's making fun of me!"

"They do that." Dad turned to me and said, "We're going to wish Bill luck before the show. Aren't you at least riding in the boat with the boys?"

"Ha! I'd rather go shopping." Snort.

As Frances pushed open the door into the sunshine, she said something in Russian. Something long that she was determined to get out in full. Dad stood in the doorway and waited for her with a look of pure luv while she finished.

I didn't need any sage advice on honesty and I *definitely* didn't need any from Dostoyevsky. "*Do svidanya*," I muttered. Then I realized the customer from across the showroom was approaching the counter. "Yes ma'am, may I help—" It was Tammy.

She slid a candy bar onto the counter. "Hook me up, would you? Now that I have a boyfriend, I'm trying to maintain my girlish figure."

As I scanned the candy into the register, I looked over my shoulder to see whether Mrs. Vader was listening from the office. I'd told customers off before when Mrs. Vader wasn't around, if they really deserved it. Tammy was McGillicuddy's girlfriend. I didn't want to be the annoying little sister she dreaded seeing when she came over to our house. But damn if she was going to follow me around and taunt me! She could have bought a candy bar at a gas station.

She must have seen I was gearing up to tell her off. She knew me better than I'd thought. Either that or she recognized the fixed killer stare I got before I served an ace. For whatever reason, shc said in a hurry, "What draws me to McGillicuddy as a boyfriend is the same thing that draws me to you as a friend. You're both so honest, to the point of being clueless. After years of being stuck at tennis tournaments with Holly and Beige, it's refreshing."

"Eighty-three cents," I said. "You're not helping yourself here."

"And if I wanted honesty, I should have been more honest myself. When you left the party, I told McGillicuddy what I did to you. He didn't un-ask me out, but I could tell he was disappointed."

McGillicuddy would never un-ask a girl out. Even if he hated her guts, he'd keep his promise and act like a gentleman about it. I didn't tell Tammy this because she was genuinely concerned about what he thought of her now. It was sort of sweet. "If it makes you feel better," I told her, "he dreamed about you last night."

"He did?" Her face glowed in the sunlight streaming through the showroom windows. Then she quirked her eyebrows at me. "He tells you about his dreams?"

I nodded. "Me and Dad, every morning at breakfast. Are you going to pay for that?"

She dug in her pocket, peered at the change in her palm, and picked out some coins. She had the same purse-carrying issues I had. "Anyway," she said, "I'm sorry for using you. I didn't mean to hurt your feelings. I didn't give it a thought. But I should have."

"Maybe I'd like to be used by a girl." As she passed me the change, I said, "I'd like to be good enough friends with a girl that we use each other without asking, and help each other without question. I'd like to know a girl always had my back." I tossed the coins in the register and slammed the drawer shut. The nickels had slid into the dime compartment, which would drive Mrs. Vader insane.

Tammy nodded. "We'll work on it. So, the wakeboarding show's starting soon. You want to go watch it with me?"

"Can't," I said, gesturing to the crowded showroom that was my responsibility. Wait a minute—it had emptied while I wasn't watching.

Mrs. Vader popped her head out the door of the office. She gazed suspiciously at the cash register drawer, like she just *knew* something was amiss in there. "Lori, why don't you take a few hours off? You should go outside and watch the boys."

"I don't *want* to go outside and watch the boys." Actually I did. More than anything. I'd never missed a show before. And I'd never missed Adam so much. But I wanted to watch them from the roof or a tree or somewhere else Adam wouldn't see me watching them. He'd called me a bitch. I wasn't running back to him when he left me nine roses.

Mrs. Vader folded her arms. "Go outside anyway."

I folded my arms too. "I don't want to go outside."

"Well, I don't want you to work."

"I want to work."

She pointed at me and screamed like I imagined real mothers did when their daughters turned out too much like them. "You're fired!"

"All *right*!" I threw my cash register key onto the counter and stomped outside.

Then turned right back around, smacked into Tammy, stepped inside, and took the roses Mrs. Vader held out to me wrapped in a paper towel. Her lips were pressed together, just like Adam's expression when he was trying not to laugh.

I stalked down the sidewalk outside. Tammy scampered to keep up with me. "Are you really fired?"

"Of course not," I sighed. "She fires me about once a week in the summers. I guess I'll take the rest of the day off, though. What's all this for?" I slowed to a stop at the edge of the enormous crowd. The air smelled like hamburgers and funnel cakes. People stood or sat together on towels, picnicking. I could hardly see a bare patch of grass or wharf, but it wasn't quite time for the wakeboarding show.

"They're crowning the Crappie Queen!" Tammy said.

"If you're going to hang around here,

you need to use the correct pronunciation. It's *Crappy* Queen."

"It's Rachel."

Sure enough, down on the wharf, Mr. Vader was calling Rachel forward as the new Crappy Queen. There was some justice in the world.

And then I changed my mind. Instead of the evening gown I'd seen at Crappy Festivals past, Rachel skipped onto the wharf in cutoff jeans pulled over her bathing suit, and bare feet. She grinned while the outgoing Crappy Queen pinned a tiara in the shape of a fish into her hair. Maybe old Rachel was all right after all.

"Pardon," McGillicuddy said right behind me. He shoved me off the sidewalk. I shoved him back, then realized that when he pushed me, he'd tucked another rose into my bouquet. Walking backward down the hill, he blew a kiss at Tammy. Tammy giggled and blew him a kiss back.

Another voice behind me said, "A-choo!" SOMETHING FLEW INTO MY BOUQUET. I almost dropped my beautiful roses to avoid further contact with nastiness. But it was only Cameron, pretending to sneeze another rose at me.

"Racking up, aren't you?" Tammy asked, and I had to grin.

Right after Cameron came Sean. His nose was only a little blue. I could hardly tell it had bled the night before. Sean was like that. And he held a rose between his teeth.

I smirked at him. "Don't tell me. You want me to come and get it."

"Oh, no," he said through a mouthful of stem, holding up his hands in warning. "Adam would kill me." He handed me the (spitty, ew) rose. "Did Dad crown Rachel the Crappy Queen yet?"

"Yes," Tammy and I said together.

Sean's face fell. "Oh!" He ran down the sidewalk. At the bottom of the hill, he caught Rachel by the arm and talked to her for a few seconds. His face fell further, and she shook her head. He walked away after the other boys, toward the wakeboarding boat. I almost felt sorry for him.

"I'm going to congratulate Rachel on her coronation," I said to Tammy.

"You aw?" Tammy said with her mouth full of candy bar. "Uhhh—"

"Come with me, because you're my friend and help me without question. I may need someone to call 911 if she breaks my arm."

"I'w be wight behiwd woo."

I maneuvered down the hill through the crowd, using the roses to clear the way in front of me. Now Rachel talked with an elderly couple, which might make her less likely to deck me. "Rachel!" I squealed, jumping up and down, spilling petals. "Congratulations!"

She stared at me like a fish out of water, but the elderly couple thanked me in the manner of clueless grandparents, which got us out of that embarrassing little moment.

"I need to tell you a couple of things," I said, hugging the roses to my chest and putting my other arm around her.

"Come this way," Tammy said, moving along the seawall. Rachel looked back to signal the elderly couple to save her, but I moved in, blocking her view. What a team Tammy and I made. Beyond the crowd, Tammy sat on the seawall with her legs hanging over. I did the same, and Rachel sat between us.

"It wasn't my idea to enter," Rachel spoke up defensively. "I caught a two-pounder, and my granddaddy said we could *not* let the mayor's daughter win again this year with only a one-pounder and a plastic minnow."

Rachel rose further in my opinion.

"I didn't need to tell you how bizarre that is," I said. "Obviously you have a sixth sense about these things." I nodded toward Sean cranking the boat and backing it away from the wharf. My brother was in the bow, Cameron sat further back, and Adam was bent below the side of the boat, gathering something. "I needed to tell you Sean is really in love with you."

Now *she* looked toward the boat puttering across the inlet. "How do you know? You can just tell, right? You can tell by the way he acts? After the last couple of weeks, I'll never be able to trust *that* again." She tried to sound tough, but her delivery was stilted, and her eyes rolled for emphasis at the wrong place. I'd never actually talked to her before—I'd only watched her from afar—or I would have noticed this. She came off as a lot younger and more unsure of herself than I'd expected. Which made me like her even better.

"I know because he told me," I said. The boat pointed in our direction, almost like it was heading for us rather than the open water. "I also needed to tell you your wakeboard bindings came in at the showroom this morning."

"Oooh, I forgot Sean gave you a wakeboard!" Tammy said. "I wish I could learn."

"It's fun," I said. Maybe McGillicuddy could take Tammy out wakeboarding. Maybe Sean could invite Rachel again and hope she showed up this time. Of course, both Sean and McGillicuddy would have to fight the boys every step of the way. We were good together, but it would be nice to wakeboard with other people once in a while, without a freaking outcry and rumors of mutiny.

"Hey," I said suddenly. "I have a boat." There it was, tied on the side of dock in front of my house. We hardly ever used it because we were always in the Vaders' boat. I nudged Tammy. "If you want, come over after I get off work tomorrow, and I'll teach you to wakeboard." I turned to Rachel. "You too, Miss Crappy." Of course, they probably didn't have boaters' licenses, which meant I'd have to drive. They'd be learning to wakeboard, so I'd just take them around in slow circles. Surely I couldn't mess that up. They wouldn't suspect a thing.

"That would be great!" Tammy exclaimed. She touched Rachel's bare toes with her toes. "I'll pick you up, Your Crappiness."

In case Tammy got the wrong idea, I warned her, "McGillicuddy won't be with us. He'll be with the boys. This will be a girl trip."

"I know," she said, as if she *did* really know and wasn't trying to get out of it.

"But we could cruise by the warehouse very slowly like we need to borrow another tow rope," I said. "I have become an expert at seduction."

Rachel snorted, then gave up suppressing it and proceeded to laugh her ass off. The Crappy Crown detangled itself from her hair and would have fallen in the lake if I hadn't caught it for her. Finally she calmed enough to cough out, "I don't know. I'm not very graceful."

"Who am I," I asked, "Michelle Kwan?"

"Not hardly," Tammy said at the same time Rachel said, "I see your point." But neither of them was looking at me. They watched the wakeboarding boat float right in front of us, full of boy.

Specifically, full of Adam. He stood in the bow, one arm cradling a bouquet of roses—a funny contrast, this muscular football player carrying pink flowers. He held his other hand out to me.

McGillicuddy leaned over the bow, too, and caught the seawall, holding the boat there so it didn't scrape against the wall and didn't drift away. The boys had planned ahead. For once.

Ninety-nine percent of me leaped up immediately and knocked Adam over, hugging him. One percent was still bitter about the bitch comment, and angry that I'd been tricked into coming out here to wait like some airhead flirt for Adam to happen by. This one percent was heavier than the rest combined and anchored me to the seawall. I elbowed Tammy. "Traitor."

"I was helping you without question," she said.

"And your mom!" I yelled to Adam. "Did you ask your mom to get me out here?"

"I told her to fire you if she had to," he called. "Did she fire you?"

"Mama Vader has some feminine wiles!" I exclaimed.

Adam laughed. "She's got maybe one more feminine wile than you, and you've got about three-fourths of a wile." He tilted his head and wiggled the fingers of his outstretched hand. "Come with us. We want you to close the show. Right, Sean?"

"Right!" Sean said with fake enthusiasm. From the back of the boat, Cameron waved my wakeboard at me to show me, again, that they'd thought ahead.

"I'm not supposed to get my stitches wet," I reasoned.

"Don't fall," Adam reasoned right back.

I wanted to go. I couldn't quite detach the heavy one percent. "You called me a bitch. I'm not running back to you when you leave me a dozen roses."

"Four more." He waved his smaller bouquet at me. "Sixteen total. Birthday or what?"

Rachel shoved me forward—which, since I was sitting down, didn't push me into the boat. It only folded me over like a movie theater seat.

"You can think about it," Adam said. "The four of us can take our turns, and we'll come back to see if you've changed your mind. But I want you to come with us now." In a singsong voice he coaxed, "I'll let you drive."

McGillicuddy and Cameron stared at Adam, eyes wide with fear. Sean coughed, "Bullshit."

"I'll let you drive when *I'm* wakeboarding, anyway," Adam said.

"It's love," McGillicuddy said, motioning with his head for me to get in the boat. "Let Tammy hold your roses so they don't go bald in the wind."

McGillicuddy's blessing was the final push I needed. I held out my arms for the extra roses from Adam and inhaled one last long sniff before handing off the whole huge bouquet to Tammy. Then I took Adam's hand and let him help me in. McGillicuddy shoved the bow away from the seawall and walked into the back of the boat, muttering, "Freaking femme fatale."

As we puttered out of the idle zone, I gave Rachel and Tammy a pageant wave. They waved back and clapped for me. The boat reached the open water and sped up. The motor and Nickelback drowned out the clapping. Adam grabbed my waving hand, and we did the secret handshake.

As we sank to the bow seat, I touched

his skull-and-crossbones pendant on a new leather string. "They still have these in the bubblegum machine?"

"Sean went under the dock and found it for me."

I nodded. "He was the best choice to rescue it for you. He has no fear of bryozoa." Squinting into the sun behind Adam, I looked up into his sky-blue eyes. "One day on the boat when we were kids, did you tell me you wanted me to be your girlfriend when we were old enough?"

He slid his hand down a lock of my hair and twisted it around his fingers. "I don't remember saying that, but I wouldn't be surprised. I wasn't lying that day in the truck. I really have loved you forever. Why else would I wear a skull-and-crossbones necklace you bought me from a bubblegum machine? It turned my skin green."

"It didn't." To make sure, I moved the pendant aside and peered at his chest, which looked the normal scrumptious tan to me. "It didn't," I repeated with more confidence.

"It did when you first gave it to me. Any metal coating that might have been clinging to it wore off on my chest years ago."

Come to think of it, the pendant *was* a funny color not found in nature. I'd probably given him lead poisoning, which was why he acted like that. I ran my fingertips down the bones, and poked the skull in the eyes. "You know, you could have told me you loved me a long time ago, before things got so crazy."

"No, I couldn't. I like to take chances. I'd blow a chance on anything but you. You didn't love *me*."

Didn't I? It was hard to believe I'd called him *little dolphin* just two weeks before. "I didn't think about you that way. Clearly I was capable of it. Because I love you now."

He grinned and took my hand. "We should add another step to the secret handshake."

"Then we couldn't do it in public." I turned his hand over and ran my fingertip lightly over his palm until he shivered. "When Sean came up to your mom because a fish had mouthed his toe, and my mom said I should just wait until I was sixteen . . . That wasn't Sean. That was you. Right?"

He put his head close to mine, watching my finger trace valentines in his open hand.

"I didn't want you to like me because you thought you were supposed to. I wanted you to like me for me." His breathing sounded funny. He was about to cry—which was going to cause him a world of trouble with the boys. He could live the first time down owing to the shock of seeing me crash into a very large, very stationary object. But if he cried again, he was toast.

I knew one way to stop him. I hollered above the motor, "Oh my God, Adam, are you about to *cry*?"

"Oh my God!" Sean echoed in a high-pitched girl-voice. Cameron squealed, "Adam, don't cry!" My brother called, "No crying on the boat."

Adam laughed with tears in his eyes and kissed me softly on the forehead, the side away from the stitches. And suddenly, to my complete horror, *I* was the one crying, sobbing into his chest. I was happy, but that wasn't why I was crying. I was relieved. Relieved of a weight I couldn't even name.

He held me more tightly and kissed my forehead several more times, then made his way down my cheek, dangerously close to my ear. I giggled at the same time I cried. If he didn't stop, he was going to give me hiccups—which would be so incredibly sexy, on top of messing up my timing for wakeboarding jumps.

He kissed my lips. "What do you want to do tonight?" he whispered.

What a question!

"Put our names back on the bridge," I said. "Only, you hold the sailboat this time, and I'll take care of the handwriting." I took a deep breath and let it out slowly, enjoying the warmth of Adam's arms around me against the wind. We sat back and watched the other boats and the crowded banks of the lake spin by. When the show started, we spotted for the other boys while they took their turns. Then it was Adam's turn, and mine.

About the Author

Jennifer Echols grew up on beautiful Lake Martin in Alabama and learned to waterski when she was five years old—wakeboarding wasn't invented yet! She's also the author of *Major Crush*, about a beauty queen turned band geek in a small southern town. Currently she lives with her husband and son in Birmingham, Alabama. Please visit her online at www.jennifer-echols.com or e-mail her at echolsjenn@yahoo.com.

LOL at this sneak peek of

In the Stars

By Stacia Deutsch and Rhody Cohon

A new Romantic Comedy from Simon Pulse

I've lost my mother's diamond. Not the whole ring, mind you, just the diamond.

Cherise says it's a sign.

"A sign of what?" I ask.

"A sign of your future." There's an eerie golden gleam in her dark brown eyes. "It's a sign that true love is coming your way."

"Yeah, right," I snort. Not a ha-ha funny snort, but a full-throttle, you-are-out-of-your-mind kind of snort. "You crack me up."

Cherise snorts back at me. Only louder and better. Her snort actually echoes off the walls of the school hallway, bouncing locker to locker until some freshman girls at the end of the hall turn to see what the racket's all about. They glance nervously in our direction then rush off to class.

We look at each other and both start laughing. It's absolutely hysterical that the girls ran off. If they'd just hung out a little longer, they would have discovered that Cherise is not the type to harm the young. Quite the opposite, in fact. She's all about love and peace and cosmic harmony. Cherise was born in the wrong decade. She should have been a flower child of the sixties.

Cherise Gregory has been my best friend since kindergarten and lives in the apartment above mine. When she's not attending rallies for gender equality or animal rights, Cherise's favorite pastime is finding signs in the universe and interpreting their meaning.

You might wonder why Cherise and I are friends at all. I like factual, hard science and keeping my feet grounded in the reality of what's happening today, not what might be someday. Whereas Cherise lives for tomorrow and side-trips into metaphysical fantasy.

We may seem entirely different on the surface, but once you get to know us, you'll see that Cherise and I have lots of things in common. And for those things we don't have in common, well, that's what makes our friendship interesting.

I've always thought that we're good together because we balance each other out.

We both love hangin' at the Corner Café (it's like our home away from home), reading romance novels (Cherise takes them seriously, I just think they're fun), watching classic movies (we especially like the ones with happy endings), and, of course, looking up at the stars. We are both really into the stars. The big dif is that we come at our passion for the nighttime sky from different perspectives: Cherise is into hoo-ha voodoo astrology, whereas I prefer the academic pursuit of astronomy.

Don't get me wrong, I'm really supportive when Cherise uses astrology to forecast the weather, intuit what questions will be on our exams, or make personal decisions like if she should buy the black or the brown clogs. On the flip side, she's infinitely patient when I regale her with some little-known fact about the molecular makeup of Saturn's rings or feel the burning need to share pictures of the Eagle Nebula. We each have our own perspective on the stars and we're fine with our differences. I would even say it enhances our friendship . . . most of the time.

I've never tried to press Cherise to take a more scholarly approach to the planetary system, and only once before has Cherise ever dared to make a prediction about anything connected to my personal life. It was seven years ago, and neither of us has ever mentioned it since. That's why it's incredibly odd that today she's interpreting the loss of my mother's diamond as something more than what it is: the accidental loss of a valuable, sentimental stone.

"It's definitely a cosmic marker," Cherise reiterates as I grab my books for class and a bottle of water from my locker before flinging it shut. The doorjamb is bent. I have to slam the door over and over again to finally get it closed.

"I don't really see how losing the diamond out of my mother's ring can be a signal of impending romance," I say as I twist the combination lock, mixing up the numbers. "Really, Cherise, you sound like a bad fortune cookie."

"You know I'm right." Cherise closes her locker smoothly. It clicks shut, but she doesn't twist the lock. She leaves it unlocked, preferring to trust in the goodness of human nature instead. So far, no one has stolen from her.

"Sylvie, you aren't in tune with the

universe," Cherise tisks, while we head down the hall toward the one class we take together, English literature. "Good thing for you, *I* am." She grins. "It's so obvious. Diamonds are the stone of engagement. Engagement is what inevitably happens to a couple in love. When you find the right guy, he'll give you a diamond of your very own." She seems quite sure of herself. "Losing your mother's diamond means that the right guy is coming soon. Really, really soon." Cherise smiles widely. Her straight teeth are a reminder of the years we suffered through braces together. "I have no doubt. Love is headed your way, Sylvie Townsend."

"ONCE UPON A TIME"

is timely once again as fresh, quirky heroines breathe life into classic and much-loved characters.

Renowned heroines master newfound destinies, uncovering a unique and original **"happily ever after. . . ."**

BEAUTY SLEEP
Cameron Dokey

MIDNIGHT PEARLS
Debbie Viguié

SNOW
Tracy Lynn

WATER SONG
Suzanne Weyn

THE STORYTELLER'S DAUGHTER
Cameron Dokey

BEFORE MIDNIGHT
Cameron Dokey

GOLDEN
Cameron Dokey

THE ROSE BRIDE
Nancy Holder

From Simon Pulse
Published by Simon & Schuster